BERKELEY PUBLIC LIBRARY
Date Due

DEC 20 1994			
JAN 26 1995			
FEB 27 1995			
MAR 20 1995			
JUN 13 1995			
SEP 16 1995			
SEP 29 1995			

recycled paper

NOV 15 '94

A Lonely Devil

A Lonely Devil

Sousa Jamba

FOURTH ESTATE · *London*

First published in Great Britain in 1993 by
Fourth Estate Limited
289 Westbourne Grove
London W11 2QA

A catalogue record for this book is available from the British Library.

ISBN 1-85702-049-9

Typeset by York House Typographic Ltd, London
Printed in Great Britain by Biddles Ltd, Guildford and King's Lynn

For William Mount

*M*y story is of a man who set out on a quest for love and innocence. I have always wanted to be loved by everyone. I have always wanted to be surrounded by people whose affection I could take for granted. I have always yearned for a time when I would not have to prove myself as a good citizen, as a worthy lover.

My mother never loved me; she sent me to an orphanage when I was four. My father never loved me; he hanged himself when I was ten. The nuns and maids at the orphanage where I grew up were angelic; but there were too many of us vying for their love. I have made love to many women both physically and in my imagination, but I never felt loved by any of them, never felt that if I ceased to exist it would make the slightest difference to their lives.

It is the search for love that will sustain me in writing this story. I will pour out my heart and hope that some will empathise with me. I hope that some will even come to love me. I know it is a lot to ask, since I may not seem lovable. It might, indeed, seem absurd that a man such as myself, capable of the most frightful acts, should long for love. My life has been a succession of absurdities. There is much that I have done for which I cannot account. There are so many stains on my life *that some people may feel I should be prepared to suffer eternal damnation. I hope, however, that many will realise that even the most odious being on earth was once a baby, and yearns for some affection.*

1

Roots

My mother was a short woman of medium build, with very large, dark eyes. Her parents were from Diaz city, the capital of Henrique, my native African island. She had long, dark hair, which she always wore in intricate plaits. She had a very sharp voice. I do not know whether this is an exact description of her; however, that is how she remains engraved on my memory. There was a time, when I was a small baby, when my mother loved me. Some people told me later that, unlike other babies, I never used to cry. They told me that my mother would often leave me at her friend's house and I would remain in complete silence.

Memories of my childhood are all confined to the orphanage in Diaz city. Catholic nuns ran the orphanage, which consisted of a large white house with two dormitories. The girls – there were very few of them – had a dormitory of their own. At the age of ten, I moved to another dormitory where several older boys were living. Brother Juan, a Spaniard who spoke a mixture of

Spanish and Portuguese, supervised the dormitory. We all liked Brother Juan. He made sure that we attended school and that we involved ourselves in sports: he was obsessed with volley-ball, football, table tennis. Brother Juan, as everyone kept saying, trained Vicente Correia, the only Henriquean to have played for a first-division Portuguese team. The oldest boy in the orphanage – who is now exiled in Angola – was seventeen. His name was Miguel Valente. Brother Juan was very fond of Miguel.

It was at the orphanage that the feeling of being inadequate settled into me. I used to wet the bed. The maids who cleaned our dormitory always reported me to Brother Juan; some of them even cursed me. Brother Juan would take me aside and remind me to 'have a pee' always before going to bed. I also made a point of not drinking anything last thing at night. This did not help; other boys laughed at me. Some suggested that I should have a frog tied to my waist; others that I should be flogged. I hated myself all that time. Sometimes, I would go to a private place and cry because I wanted to stop wetting the bed. One evening, Dona Guilhermina, who came to the orphanage to help with the work there, found me crying. She called me to her side and asked what was bothering me. I told her.

She said, 'Nando, I am sure you will soon stop wetting the bed because you are going to wake up in the middle of the night and walk straight to the toilet.'

Dona Guilhermina saved me. I woke up every night, defied the bogeymen who lingered between the lavatory and our dormitory; and Fernando Luis lost the tag of the bed-wetter. One day, Brother Juan gave me a table-tennis racket as a prize for my effort. I became very attached to Dona Guilhermina. Other boys were close to the nuns, and I had a strong feeling that the nuns did not like me as much as them. It was Dona Guilhermina who taught me how to sew a button to a shirt. She also taught me how to put a hem on a pair of shorts. Whenever she saw me, Dona Guilhermina would give me a kiss and a hug. Sometimes, I sought her out just for a chat. All our activities at the orphanage interested Dona Guilhermina.

I attended the local Catholic school, Our Lady of Conception, which was in the middle of Diaz city, within walking distance of the orphanage. Though I was not a poor pupil, I was certainly not the best: anything to do with numbers frightened me. I did, however, enjoy composition. When we were asked to write a long essay about 'The person I admire most', I chose Dona Guilhermina. I went to her and asked her about her family, her work and her opinions. My teacher thought my essay was so good that she typed it and pinned it on the notice-board.

Brother Juan, who taught Physical Education at the school, decided that we should start a small wall news-paper. He took charge of it. I was thirteen at the time. The wall newspaper was a success. We wrote about events in Diaz city. We would give the articles to Rito, who had very legible handwriting, and he would copy them out on white paper that we would stick on the wall. As soon as the latest edition of the paper was glued to the wall, people would gather around it. That was when I discovered the power of journalism. I was thrilled by the thought that people actually believed what I had written; it gave me immense power.

Even then, I already felt lonely. I wanted to be heard, and through writing I felt that I could reach people. My colleagues producing the newspaper lost their enthusiasm and it ceased to be. But I never lost my love for journalism.

Several incidents at the orphanage filled me with anger. From the time that I was aware of my own singularity I knew that I carried evil within me. I knew I could never love people as much as I would have wanted.

There was a boy in our dormitory called Roberto, who must have been two years my senior. Roberto was very popular with the boys because he always impersonated Brother Juan and his Spanish accent. Besides being an able mimic, Roberto played the guitar, the trumpet and the marimba. He was also a good dancer and he could run very fast. Whatever he did, Roberto was certain to come out top. Unlike me, Roberto was very handsome: the maids called him 'the boy with the fine looks'. Roberto had no flaws, and this saddened me a lot. In class, he often came top. His Portuguese was impeccable. One Christmas, Roberto declaimed to a gathering of the local colonial officers a long speech in Latin, which Brother Juan had given him. He got prolonged applause and whistles. Yet when I declaimed a poem about the Tagus on the same occasion I only received polite, modest clapping.

Roberto was so talented on the guitar that he would give his own little concerts. The other boys would gather around and he would sing popular songs or ones he had just composed. No event of note in the dormitory passed without Roberto composing a song about it. One night, after eating some horrible fish, we were all seized by diarrhoea. As we stood in a queue, shouting at the person in the WC to be quick, one boy exclaimed, 'Oh, this is the end.' Roberto's song was also called 'This is the end' and brought tears of laughter to the eyes of many boys. I, however, kept hoping that something bad would happen to Roberto. I hated him.

Sister Aluveva, who was in charge of the orphanage, only allowed us to go to the beach with Brother Juan. One day at the beach, while all the other boys were playing football some distance away, I found myself lying next to Roberto, who had brought his guitar. Saying that he was not feeling well, Roberto lay down and fell into a deep sleep. I seized his guitar, put it in the water and let it float away on the waves. I then rushed to where the other boys were.

Minutes later, Roberto came up in tears: 'My guitar, my guitar, it's gone with the water. Brother Juan, the guitar is gone.'

Everyone ran to the point where I had put the guitar into the sea. It had by then floated so far, we could see only a glimpse of it. Brother Juan plunged into the water at once to get it. He swam for a long time, but had to give up because it had drifted too far. Roberto was crying, saying he would never have a guitar again. He kept saying someone must have put the guitar in the water while he was asleep. All the other boys tried to console him. I was overwhelmed with joy. I was so pleased that I gave out a little giggle.

Luckily enough, only one person, Lidio, noticed. He said, 'I don't see anything funny in this.'

I said, 'Well, if he's so clever why did he let his damned guitar float away?'

Lidio told me to shut up and walked away, over to the other boys. When Brother Juan got out of the water, he put his arms around Roberto and told him not to cry. I was pleased that Roberto no longer had the guitar. I was also pleased at seeing him look so sad and weakened. This was not the self-confident boy who could sing in French, but one whose eyes were filled with tears. Sister Aluveva soon bought Roberto a new guitar. This saddened me a lot. He also started playing the piano. Everyone said Roberto was destined to succeed.

There was, however, a pleasant surprise in waiting: Roberto caught some disease, which left him not only paralysed but, to my immense pleasure, half blind.

However hard I tried, I never became popular with the other boys. We had a very good football pitch. Brother Juan spent hours supervising the workmen who maintained it. He organised football matches between us and other teams. I was not in our team because I hated football. In fact, I hated all sports. One day when our team was playing a game of crucial importance Banquinho, the goalkeeper, fell ill with some kind of fever. Since no one wanted to be goalie, Banquinho approached me to stand in for him. He said this was my chance to become popular with the others; there were still many people who viewed me as the bed-wetter. I told Banquinho – whose real name was Armando Bento – that I was hopeless at football, but he insisted that I had a go. I gave in at last. To my own surprise, I turned out to be very good in the first half. One goal went through, but not even the best goalkeeper on the island would have managed to contain that shot. By half-time we were drawn; the score was 1–1. Our team was truly impressive, but our opponents – a group of boys from the Castelo area – were no turnips, as we said. Our rivals were determined to prove that they were our equals. They were very disciplined and none of them held on to the ball for long: they kept our team on the defensive for most of the time. Then, as Brother Juan was about to signal the end of the game, I let one goal through. It was all my fault; I had been slightly absent-minded. The other team was overjoyed. The Diaz Angels, as we called our team, had been routed. My team mates began to grumble that had Banquinho been around this would not have happened. I hated myself. I wished I could have thrown myself into the sea and let sharks eat me up so I would never be seen again.

That evening at supper time everyone kept cursing me, questioning why they had not made a better choice for a substitute goalkeeper.

Sister Aluveva made a point of giving each of us a present on our birthday. In return, we all gave her a present on her birthday. On my fourteenth birthday, 25th October, Sister Aluveva gave me a copy of *Os Maias* by Eica de Queiroz, a classic that she said would give me an opportunity to wander into the celestial world of Portuguese literature. I left it on my bed and went off for Catechism. When I came back, the book was gone. I looked everywhere, but I could not find it. I reported this to Brother Juan, who went to tell Sister Aluveva that the book had been stolen.

Sister Aluveva was red-faced with anger when she came to our dormitory. She ordered us all to assemble and she gave us a long talk about the evils of jealousy and theft. She asked the perpetrator of the crime to confess and hand over the book to her at once. No one did. She said if no one came forward then everyone would be punished: there would be no games or visits to the beach. She said there were also other punishments in store. I was the only person who was exempted from them.

A day after Sister Aluveva had ordered the punishment, I found my copy of *Os Maias*. I had forgotten that I had left it in my locker. However, I did not tell either Brother Juan or Sister Aluveva that I had found the book. I wanted everyone to be punished. In fact, I hid the book under my mattress, where I thought no one would find it.

After four days, the boys were grumbling. They all suspected that Rito, who had stolen before, had done it again. As they remained in the dormitory reading instead of going out to play football, the boys kept telling Rito to hand over the book. Rito kept professing his innocence. One boy even said he was sure he had seen Rito trying to sell the book. I often went up to Rito and insulted him, calling him a worthless thief.

Rito would say, 'Nando, the truth will come out one day. I am innocent.'

We went in a delegation to Sister Aluveva and said that we were certain Rito had stolen my book. Sister Aluveva responded by saying she was going to give him only half his pocket-money until she had deducted enough for another copy of *Os Maias*. There was joy that afternoon in the dormitory when everyone learnt that the punishment was over. We called Rito all sorts of names. Everyone said he should have confessed straight away that he had stolen the book. Still, Rito professed his innocence. This angered Brother Juan, who insisted that Rito show some sign of remorse. At last, Rito accepted that he had stolen the book and he apologised in front of all the other boys. As he said that he was sorry, he looked at me straight in the eyes and began to cry. In the days that followed, Rito was often to be seen by himself.

One day, Sister Aluveva came and gave me another copy of *Os Maias*; she gave Rito a beautiful Bible and a flute, as well as some beautiful-looking cards on which to write apologies to us all. After that, everyone forgave him: that is, except me. In fact, he was soon more popular than I was because of his flute; in no time, he had learnt to play several tunes.

Hearing about the missing book, Dona Guilhermina went to the island's main bookshop and bought a copy of *Os Maias*. Then she summoned both Rito and me, gave me the copy of *Os Maias* and asked me to forgive Rito. She told us to shake hands and to say to each other that we were going to be friends. I complied, and Rito repeated the words after me; but he cried some more.

I now had three copies of *Os Maias*. Sometimes, I would watch as Rito sat alone in complete silence. I wished that he would roast in hellfire. I felt that he had wronged me. I hated him.

The maids reported to Sister Aluveva that they had found some cigarette stubs in the toilet. Sister Aluveva stormed into our dormitory one evening and ordered us all to stand on one side; she was going to search our lockers. I wished I could die, knowing I now had three copies of *Os Maias* tucked away beneath my shirts. Sister Aluveva and Brother Juan found nothing that was forbidden in the lockers. In fact, some of the articles they found made the dormitory rock with laughter: a bottle of honey hidden in a shoe-box; a little sack containing toy soldiers and racing cars; a maize cob; and a bottle of some soft drink. Neither Sister Aluveva nor Brother Juan asked the boys in whose lockers these items were found to account for them.

When they came to my locker they found the three copies of *Os Maias* – including the one I claimed had been stolen.

Sister Aluveva opened the front pages of the books and saw the two that she had dedicated to me. She looked straight at me and assumed a serious expression. Everyone was staring.

I said, 'Rito, I am sorry.'

There were murmurs in the dormitory.

Brother Juan walked over to me and said, 'Nando, why did you do that?'

'I don't know. I am very sorry, Brother Juan.'

Sister Aluveva was a hefty woman who rode a motorcycle and chopped firewood; people said she could kill pigs with her bare hands. She rushed straight for me and held me by the left ear. She dragged me out of the dormitory into her office and told me to sit down on the floor.

'This is one of the most evil deeds I have ever seen here in the orphanage,' she began. 'Do you realise the pain you must have caused to everyone?'

'Yes, Sister.'

'Why did you do it, for the love of God?'

'I don't know.'

'Do you realise that what you've done is evil?'

'Yes, Sister, I know it is evil.'

'Did you know that you were being evil when you did it?'

'Yes, Sister.'

The following day, I was to start my punishment. I had to remain near Sister Aluveva's office for most of the afternoon and was given little errands: to clean her office, pick up the papers in the yard, clean the windows or tend the garden. Sister Aluveva sometimes helped me when I was working in the garden. One day, she even kissed me for having done such good work.

My reputation in the dormitory was very bad; everyone held me in low esteem. I knew the other boys made jokes about me in my absence. I felt completely ostracised. I was, however, eventually forgiven when Sister Aluveva gave me cards on which I had to write apologies to everyone in the dormitory. Unlike Rito, who had written the same words in all the cards, I wrote different things for each person, as they discovered by comparing their cards.

One afternoon, I went into the cathedral by myself to pray. I wanted to ask God to make me a good person, to wash away all the evil that dwelled in me. I felt helpless. There were several elderly women lighting candles at the entrance. The stained-glass windows filled the whole large building with holy rays. Statues of the Virgin Mother and other saints were watching me. I gazed at the statue of the Virgin Mother for a long time. Sister Aluveva had just imported it from Portugal, since the previous statue had been broken during a procession through the main avenue in Diaz city. Many Henriqueans insisted that the two men who had been carrying the statue had been drunk. I knelt silently in the pews and begged God to make me a good man. I promised I would never again be as evil as I had been to Rito. I earnestly believed that God had heard me.

Although I had ostensibly been pardoned by the other boys, I still felt that in their hearts they hated me for what I had done. I even hated myself because I knew I had enjoyed seeing them being punished and had longed for a time when I could punish them myself. I hated myself for delighting in other people's pain.

My behaviour at the orphanage showed me quite early that evil was embedded in me.

I was still at the orphanage when Henrique became independent. I was then sixteen. I still remember that day in 1975 when the flag of the Henriquean Liberty Movement, the party to which all nationalists had belonged, was hoisted. Machado Alves, the general secretary of the MHL, was proclaimed president. Diaz city resounded to the sound of drums on Independence Day. People danced till they could do so no more. Henrique was free at last. The nuns, led by Sister Aluveva, said they were not going to leave Henrique. However, two months after independence, the authorities closed down the orphanage where I had been for twelve years.

Marxism was then in fashion: everyone who had ever read a book tried to out-Marx Marx. In those days, there was no better compliment that could be bestowed on anyone than to describe him as belonging to the extreme left. People breathed Marxism. It was as though this euphoria was never going to wane. Party militants often ridiculed Christians. I recall a time when the youth wing of the MHL marched in the streets of Diaz city calling for the closure of the cathedral.

After leaving the orphanage, I managed to get a job working for *Luz*, the only newspaper in the country. Here, as elsewhere in Henrique, the Monangolas – the most powerful clan on the island – predominated.

For us Henriqueans, ancestry mattered a lot because it determined one's position in the society. There were three main clans on the island: the Monangolas, the Congos, and the Ngungas. The Monangolas were said to be descended from a group of plantation workers from Angola. The Congos were said to be descended from the Congo Republic. The Ngungas are said to have been the original inhabitants of the island. Then, there were many rootless people, like me, in Diaz city and Pololo, the island's two main cities. For us, the rootless, there was a limit to how far we could go. At *Luz*, for instance, I could never become a senior editor, a post then held by Diego Reis, an incompetent drunk. As a rootless person, my sole importance at *Luz* was that I had a certain facility with words and could, therefore, be slightly more effective in peddling whatever line the authorities required of us.

When I began to work at *Luz*, I shared a house with three other young people – Jaime, Rodolfo and Walter – who worked in some government offices. They drank a lot, but they were very good cooks. We took turns at cooking, so I asked Dona Guilhermina to teach me to make some dishes. She taught me how to cook bacalhau with rice, salads, fish and meat. However, when I tried to put into practice what I had learnt, my house-mates were not prepared to taste what I cooked, claiming that they would have preferred pig-feed. One day, I took the dish I had made to Dona Guilhermina who insisted that it was all right. I was convinced that my house-mates hated me because I had come from an orphanage and lacked a proper background.

I felt forsaken, and saw no need to harbour any love in my heart. I had forgotten all the vows I had made in the cathedral. I had become myself again.

Rodolfo and Walter were of the Monangola clan, the dominant clan on the island. Every weekend, local girls, none of them Monangolas, filled our house. These girls came to chat, to drink beer or to listen to music on Rodolfo's sophisticated hi-fi equipment. Like all Monangolas, Rodolfo and Walter treated the girls as – went the saying – 'mattress fodder'. One Sunday afternoon, Rodolfo coupled with three different girls. Whenever they could, Rodolfo and Walter coupled with the girls after getting them drunk.

However, when they were in the company of girls from the Monangola clan they showed due respect and did not try anything that would have demeaned them. In that company I felt inferior, not being a Monangola, much like that mattress fodder. I was trash. I found many of the girls – the trash – quite repulsive. These were girls who could drink a whole bottle of whisky without seeming drunk. They had a very strange form of contraception. Rodolfo and Walter told me that, after the act, the girls would stuff themselves with aspirins and then wash. There were many bad stories about these girls.

I dreamt of going out with a real Monangola girl. I did not want anyone in Henrique to associate me with the Henriquean trash. Monangola men who were married to women from some other clan could beat their wives at will; Henriqueans almost expected it. However, if a man from some other clan who was involved with a Monangola woman were to slap her, it was as though the whole clan had been insulted. For those of us with no background, getting involved with a Monangola was a step towards the centre of power.

What, then, was my background? Why was I almost rootless? Why had my mother sent me to the orphanage? After I had already been working at *Luz* for some time, Dona Guilhermina invited me over one afternoon to tell me about my roots.

Dona Guilhermina was short and – some would say – stumpy. She had a little beard. I recall her always being dressed in black; she had so many relatives on the island that she seemed to be in permanent mourning. However, she was always laughing and her house was always filled with young people. She is the only woman I have known who was always whistling, even when she walked in the street, as though she were a man. She had mothered thirteen children (which, on our island, was not an outstanding feat), most of whom had left home and gone to different parts of the island and abroad.

That afternoon, I had felt very tired at *Luz*; my office, which was separate from the editorial floor, had poor ventilation and I felt very sticky. I was eager to get to Dona Guilhermina's house because she said she had something important to tell me.

As I now recall that afternoon as I walked to Dona Guilhermina's many aspects of Henrique come to my mind. There was a strong smell coming from the kitchens – of fish being cooked, plantain being boiled, shrimps being fried in palm oil – which mingled with the smell of rotting garbage, urine and general decay. The singing of children in the neighbourhood filled the air. In that mêlée, I could discern the sound of shortwave radios; their owners must have been hoping something about the island that they did not know would finally be said. As I came closer to Dona Guilhermina's house, there were drunks having heated arguments about sports.

Dona Guilhermina's house was at one end of Diaz city. A Portuguese family had owned the house in which she lived and had handed it over to Dona Guilhermina before leaving for Portugal. Like most houses on the island, it had a high ceiling, a floor made of concrete and there was a long corridor. It was a house built to fight the sun and humidity. The house was built on elevated land to capture any breeze. It felt very fresh. Dona Guilhermina was ironing when I arrived there.

'Fernando!' she exclaimed, as I stood before the veranda.

'Good afternoon, Dona,' I replied.

We sat on the veranda, which overlooked the sea. Dona Guilhermina offered me a can of Coca-Cola and continued ironing. As she ironed, she said she had always wanted to tell me about my life. She said she had always felt that women on the island who had known my mother owed me an explanation about how I had come into being. Dona Guilhermina said she had watched me closely as I grew up at the orphanage and then moved to *Luz*.

I had heard snatches about my background, but it had never been so clear as when Dona Guilhermina unfurled it before me. I sat still while she spoke in a subdued voice.

Dona Guilhermina said Marta – for that was my mother's name – had been a girl of much promise in her time. In those days, sailors used to stop in Diaz city on their way to Angola from the north of Brazil and Portugal. An enterprising Portuguese trader called Jose had set up a restaurant and held shows to entertain the sailors. That was where my mother's talent as a singer was discovered. My mother sang the fado, and the samba tunes that were then the rage in Brazil. All of Henrique, Dona Guilhermina said, was at that time taken up by music and dance. The sailors who saw my mother sing in Jose's restaurant were impressed, and they had all said that if only my mother were to go to Brazil or Portugal she would have had a remarkable career. My mother dreamt of becoming a samba star. Some people on the island had even started referring to her as Marta, the samba girl. All the men wished to befriend my mother.

My grandparents had not approved of my mother's activities. They believed that she should marry, become a proper housewife and follow the lifestyle befitting a person of her background. That is, to be a maid to the Portuguese families on the island, a cook or laundry woman. Then my mother fell pregnant with me. Everyone began to speculate about who the father might be. But despite the many suggestions, no one knew for sure. My mother would not say. She tried to get rid of me. Dona Guilhermina said all my mother's efforts at aborting me failed: I persisted in coming into this world.

My birth had a negative effect on my mother's singing career, because she spent most of her time looking after me. Both my grandparents died within a few months of each other. Then, when I was four, an Angolan band came to perform on the island and my mother travelled with them around the island. They occasionally let her sing with them. My mother became a star once again. When the band returned to Angola, she decided to go along with them. She dumped me in the local orphanage. My mother was never heard of again. Some people later said she had become an alcoholic and drunk herself to death.

Dona Guilhermina coughed and said, 'But your mother's real dream was to become a samba artist. Oh,

21

she was crazy about samba! Ah, Marta, the girl who loved the samba!'

'What about my father?' I asked.

Dona Guilhermina said she was one of the few people who had known for certain who my father was. Having been close to my mother, she had been told. Dona Guilhermina reminded me of an incident that I remembered very clearly: it had occurred when I was ten. As she told me about it, I recalled every minute of that day.

It had been a Sunday afternoon. The citizens of Diaz were out in their best clothes. Many people had gone to the beach; Henriqueans loved the beach. I had been feeling lonely and alienated at the time. The nuns and the maids at the orphanage were gentle and caring, but I had begun to feel slightly estranged from them. Now and then, although it was not yet clear to me, I had started to ponder my future. Many of my school-mates used to talk about their dreams. Some of them even talked about their parents. It was strange. We were at the orphanage because our parents had been unable to look after us, and yet most boys were always going on about their mothers and fathers. That Sunday afternoon, I had strayed from the orphanage and was wandering aimlessly through the streets, whiling my time away. Suddenly, I saw people rush to the western part of the city. Wondering what the interest was, I followed them. I certainly did not want to miss any spectacle.

A large crowd had gathered around a tree. A man was hanging dead from a black electric wire tied to a branch. I had never seen a dead person before. The dead man was very handsome. He was tall, lean, and had a face with very fine features. He was dribbling. His fingers looked stiff. He had no shirt and wore brown trousers. He wore no shoes. Everyone was studying him intently, as though looking at a being from some other planet. Some of the women crossed themselves, but no one was crying. One of the men said he did not know why Cabral – that was the man's name – had decided to hang himself when they had been drinking with him only the previous day. Then a police van came, a fat Portuguese police officer came out, cut the wire from which the man was hanging, put him into the police van and drove him away to the morgue. It was then that the women began to weep. I strutted back to the orphanage and told anyone who would listen that I had seen a dead man. I was proud of having seen death.

Dona Guilhermina stopped ironing and said, 'Fernando, that Cabral Monteiro was your father. He has fathered many children on this island. Marta preferred to keep it secret rather than let the world know that she too had had a son by Cabral Monteiro.'

At first, the news that the first dead person I had ever seen was my father – and I had not known it – amused me. It seemed like some joke. But then it began to sink in. I tried to evade the truth by imagining that it was not happening to me; that all this was occurring in the life of somebody else. Alas, the truth kept forcing itself on me: as a child, I had seen my dead father. It now became clear why so many of the elderly people had looked at me and whispered to themselves. I began to hate all Henriqueans. Why had they decided to keep this information from me?

I felt sorrowful, but I could not show this to Dona Guilhermina. I wanted to show her that I was a man, a real man on whom the saddening truths of the world had little effect.

Dona Guilhermina said, 'But, Fernando, you should consider yourself lucky; at least you have done something with your life. Look at what's happened to other young people who were at the orphanage with you; they have all become complete failures.'

Looking up, Dona continued, with a dreamy expression on her face, 'God up there has been protecting you. I have been praying to Him to take care of you. Many of us have been praying for you.'

I spent the rest of the evening at Dona Guilhermina's. She kept recalling what life had been like in her days, trying hard to cheer me up. It was as though she had showered me with very cold water and now she wanted to warm me up. As I wanted to please her, I became chirpy and tried to crack some jokes. Deep in me, however, an icy reality was forming. Dona Guilhermina cooked dinner – fried fish with rice – and I ate with her. She seemed to enjoy my company. She took to me because I reminded her of her several sons who had left the island for Angola, Portugal and Mozambique.

Halfway through dinner, a lean, young woman with an oval face joined us. Her hair had been plaited intricately. She had a sharp voice. I had seen her somewhere before – at the beach perhaps. She stammered a little and laughed a lot. She spoke to Dona Guilhermina for a while about lace (she said there was a new consignment in the main shop) and the tomatoes in her mother's garden.

Dona Guilhermina turned to me and said, 'Ha, Fernando, I hope you know Teresa Sampaio.'

I shook my head. The young woman smiled nervously.

'Tete,' Dona Guilhermina said exuberantly, 'this is Fernando Luis.'

'I have seen him many times at *Luz*,' Tete said.

'Seen him in the paper or at the paper?' Dona Guilhermina asked.

'I have read some of his articles. I think I also saw him at Debora's party,' Tete replied.

Then Tete and Dona Guilhermina continued with their conversation. I was supposed to pretend that I was paying no attention to what they were discussing. I was, after all, a man. But I had a weakness: women's conversations actually interested me. At the orphanage, I had always believed that the nuns and the maids had many wonderful secrets that they were hiding from us. Tete, I soon discovered, acted as some kind of guru to Dona Guilhermina. Dona Guilhermina, unlike many elderly people in Henrique, did not want to confine her knowledge of the world to what the local media had to offer. She wanted to see the issues from different angles. She wanted to know both sides of the argument about the war in Angola and Mozambique; the question of Namibia's independence and apartheid in South Africa. Dona Guilhermina delighted in knowing the different factors that shaped events. Tete, an avid listener to radio stations and reader of magazines, for her part enjoyed giving her perspective of events to Dona Guilhermina. It occurred to me that Tete was a very dominant person. Not only did she enjoy holding court but she delighted in dinning her ideas into other people.

Suddenly, Dona Guilhermina and Tete began to discuss the Angolan war. I intervened when Tete made a statement I thought very crass: that the Angolan government needed to have discussions with its opponents. I said those fighting the Angolan regime were reactionaries on the payroll of the CIA and had to be crushed. Tete said it was not as simple as that. Dona Guilhermina followed the discussion with attentive eyes at first, but she eventually began to doze. Tete and I discussed several things: the future of our island, literature, relationships between the sexes. Tete said the government policies of collectivisation were doomed to fail; that much of the poetry written on the island was mediocre; that most of the men on the island were male chauvinists. I took to Tete at once. She reminded me of something I had always yearned for but could not quite identify. Even then, I detected a trait that was to cost her dear: speaking her mind to strangers.

Tete had just graduated from Machado Alves High School and was going to work for a while as a secondary-school teacher before leaving for Portugal to do further studies. The number of books she had already read astounded me. She was, to me, a fountain of knowledge. Dona Guilhermina shook from her sleep, and I noted that it was time for me to go. I bade my farewells and left.

After my meeting with Tete, I could not keep her out of my mind. I realised at last that this was my chance to start seeing a Monangola girl. I knew that my chances were very remote. To win Tete's heart, I would have to face stiff competition from other men who, besides being Monangolas, had other qualities that I lacked.

Two weeks later, Dona Guilhermina died of a heart attack. I felt wounded. The only person on the island who cared for me had suddenly vanished. Who would now listen to my many agonies? It was at Dona Guilhermina's funeral that I met Tete again. It was, to be precise, at the wake. Tete's voice was hoarse: she had been crying a lot. She asked me how she could get an article published in *Luz*. I told her to come to the paper to see me.

One aspect keeps coming back to my mind when I recall Dona Guilhermina's wake: the choir of women from the Protestant Church. Dona Guilhermina had converted late in life to some Protestant sect. Many people said the choir from that sect sang as though they had just descended from heaven. In those days, among the Henriquean young, religion was a risible relic of the past. Marxism was then the vogue. Many young people saw the church as something for the entertainment of elderly people. We, the young, were supposed to subscribe to dialectical materialism. The opium of the masses, the sigh of a heartless soul did not appeal to us.

Dona Guilhermina had a daughter, Alcina, who was married to Adão Jol, a member of the Section for Internal Security, the Henriquean secret police, known as the SIS. Alcina ordered the burial to be delayed, so that she could fly to Portugal to buy the proper dress for the ceremony. In Henrique, middle-class funerals were like weddings: men as well as women did everything to show off their clothes.

Three days after the wake, Tete came to *Luz*'s offices. The article she wanted to write was about male chauvinism on the island. I said I would tell the editor, Diego Reis, and would get back to her with a response.

Diego Reis could not help laughing. He said, 'I know of this Teresa Sampaio. She's a plucky little girl. Her father taught me. What she's after is a good fuck. There you are, Nando; this is your chance. Give her a good Henriquean screw and all this haughtiness will vanish.'

I said, 'Well, the screwing is certainly not out of the question, but, Comrade, this girl has some ideas of her own.'

'All women's issues have to come through the FMH,' Diego replied, referring to the Forum of Henriquean Women.

That evening, I met Tete at Beira-Mar, the main restaurant in Diaz city. I ordered a meal; Tete said she had already eaten, and settled for a bottle of beer. In colonial days, the Beira-Mar bar had been a favourite of plantation owners. Many arguments and fights had been held in it. The walls of the bar were covered with ugly paintings of scenes from the island. All the tables were filled with men talking loudly. There were very few women. In Henrique, it was not done for unaccompanied women to frequent bars and restaurants.

I said, 'I am sorry, Tete, but Diego Reis says the type of article you want will only be considered if it comes from the Women's Forum.'

'Oh, the same old rubbish,' Tete replied 'The Women's Forum is dead. The party has nothing to offer this island. All these organs meant to represent women, the youth and suchlike are mere screens for incompetence, corruption and nepotism.'

I was shocked. In Henrique, people did not criticise the party and the government so openly. After all, everyone knew of the SIS. Everyone in Henrique had heard of the East German officers who had come to endow our security policies with the efficiency and ruthlessness that, as the authorities kept saying, was necessary to keep the revolution going. It was only later that I realised why Tete was so outspoken. Like most Monangolas, she believed she had been born to rule; or, at least, to have all events under her control. Tete was not like those of us who did not have well-known families. In my case, I was a complete stranger to the people on the island who mattered – nobody knew me; nobody cared for me.

Throughout that evening at the Beira-Mar, I acted as the voice of reason, the party hack. I was sure one of the men in the restaurant was eavesdropping on our conversation. I told Tete that everything must be done in the correct fashion: an article about the comportment of Henriquean males (from a woman's point of view) had to go through the Women's Forum. After that, we discussed journalism in Henrique: Tete said the writers at *Luz* were not journalists but *fawnalists*, who spent most of their time writing pieces praising the party and not articles that reflected the reality. She spoke with passion.

That weekend, there was a party in the south-side of Diaz city. David Ramos, a central-committee member, was holding a celebration for his daughter's birthday. All the people who mattered on the island were present: political commissars, secret-police agents and smugglers. There was a lot of food and different types of drink: wine, whisky, several brands of beer. The party was almost like a festival. I had never seen so much food and splendour. This was a world those of us who did not belong to the ruling clan could only imagine. Little girls, dressed in white or pink dresses, trotted about. Little boys wore black suits and bow-ties. They all kept running towards a room where there was an ice-cream machine. The scarce foreign exchange available on the island was used to import snacks: peanuts, potato crisps, packets of pop corn and so on.

There were many glittery suits and bow-ties, which were then the rage on the island. One man, said to be a high-ranking officer in the secret police, wore a purple safari suit. Several women were dressed in yellow outfits. Their straightened hair was tied with maroon ribbons.

The most impressive woman at the party was called Nina Strasbourg. I had heard a lot about her. She was considered to be the most attractive woman the Monangola clan had ever produced. Nina Strasbourg, who had dyed her hair blonde, was wearing a black, tight-fitting velvet dress. She kept smiling, revealing a gap between her two front teeth. She danced only with people who mattered. I enjoyed just looking at her, knowing too well that were she to speak to me I would have been unable to react properly. She belonged to a completely different world. Nina, née Mateus, had worked for some Greek luxury cruise liner, on which she had fallen in love with the captain, an elderly Belgian by the name of Jean Strasbourg. When the captain retired, the two of them went to settle in the Algarve. Nina, who had ambitions to be a model, had been bored stiff. The old man died, bequeathing his extensive fortune to her. Nina went on a mad shopping spree in Lisbon and tried to become a model. None of the photographers took any note of her and she came back to Henrique. She was the island's *femme fatale*: all the men longed to go to bed with her. She married Martins Guilherme, the customs chief. It was, however, rumoured that she was having an affair with Gregorio Luvas, a local dandy.

The grandees at the party took turns at making speeches. Members of the Henriquean élite were very particular about their appearance. Purple safari suits, brown shoes and gold wristwatches were then in fashion. Speaker after speaker kept saying the birthday celebrations were a testimony to the might of the Henriquean nation. People clapped; they would have clapped at anything.

Then the dancing. The hi-fi system began to boom out zouk music and then samba. In those days, Martinho da Vila, the Brazilian samba king, was the rage. Henriqueans love to dance; everyone at the party rushed to the floor at once. After samba, it was Cape Verdean music. Rene Cabral had just released his song extolling the beauty of Cape Verdean women. Couples held each other tight as they negotiated the intricate steps of the latest dance from the Cape Verdean islands. Many people were trying a new dance that had just come from Angola in which men and women banged against each other as though practising for a session of very violent sex.

I danced with Tete for most of the night. She introduced me to her friends. She was so popular that she was even known to some ministers. I felt I had climbed up in the world. I felt important because I was now communing with the people who mattered in Henrique. I had, however, to achieve another feat: Tete's declaration of her love for me.

There was no doubt about it: I was madly in love with Tete. I am now certain that I loved Tete just for what she represented to me: social advancement. I tried, however, to convince myself that there was more that drew me to her than her social status. Her dark eyes awakened in me a longing I could not describe. Her intelligence reminded me of something that belonged to me but I did not possess. As the night wore on, slow soul music was played. The children and the elderly had all retired by then. The Master of Ceremonies said it was 'lovers' time'. Partners had all placed their heads on each other's shoulders, with dreamy expressions on their faces. I was by now slightly drunk. I felt light and there was no trace of sorrow in my mind. I was smiling. Then I kissed Tete on the lips. She smiled. She was mine. We danced till morning.

After the party, I walked Tete to her father's house. As we parted, I said, 'I love you!'

Tete replied with her eyes. They said it all: 'I love you! I need you! I adore you!'

From then on, I saw Tete almost every day. She had begun to teach Portuguese language and literature at Baixa. In the evenings, she would come to my little house and she would cook dinner. In those days, I did not have a maid. Sometimes, when work had tired her, Tete made me cook on the little gas stove. After dinner at my place, we would go to her parents' house.

Tete's father disapproved of me, of course. Senhor Sampaio was scandalised. He could not accept that his daughter – a pure Monangola through and through –

had taken up with the worst type of person on the island. To him, I was a completely rootless person. Senhor Sampaio would certainly have preferred his daughter to be seeing someone from their clan – someone who had proper Angolan blood. Senhor Sampaio, for instance, had never asked after my family. It was as though he knew the tragedy I carried in my soul.

Tete, of course, did not mind the boy from the orphanage. In fact, it gave her some kudos: by going for someone like me she had defied tradition and her own family. She felt superior to all the Monangola girls. Sometimes, we would spend the evenings chatting with her friends. She had many important friends in whose company I felt inadequate. I felt that my up-bringing had not endowed me with proper manners. I suspected that they all laughed at me when I was not around. I felt I always had to prove myself. Tete knew which families on the island mattered. They were all aware of what was done and what was considered *infra dig*. I was very lonely because in their company I felt the uninvited guest at a party.

It was almost a year into our relationship that we first made love. Tete insisted she did not want to lose her virginity before her twenty-third birthday. One evening after the desired age, Tete finally allowed me to tune her into the frequency that causes red, misty eyes in women.

At one point, she had pulled away, saying, while smiling, 'There are no orphanages in Henrique now.

Where would I dump the baby that might come from this?'

I felt so hurt that I lost my erection; it was minutes before I recovered it. Tete could often be very insensitive. I felt that sometimes she thought of me as her bauble, something she could amuse herself with. I had always suspected that Tete was not a virgin. When I looked at the sheet the following morning, there was no evidence to disprove my suspicion. I spent the following week guessing at the lucky devil who, as the saying in Henrique went, had flooded the crypt.

I was, however, a true virgin. Unlike other young men who had taken girls to the beach or to the main football stadium in Diaz city on Saturday nights, I had not even stroked a single breast. Now and then I had become close to some girl; but when I was supposed to ask her out I felt as though some powerful force took hold of my tongue. I always feared that the girl was going to tell me off. In that time, I kept, as the saying went in Henrique, honing myself for the girl of my dreams. My house-mates, who claimed to have tried all the thirty-six positions, thought of me as a complete tiro. The first time I saw Tete have an orgasm I almost ran out of the room because I thought she was going to die. As our relationship wore on, we began to experiment in bed. Tete ordered me into many quirky postures. Like most intelligent women, she wanted the act to be more than mere physical intimacy. She wanted it to be – as she often said – the physical representation of a mental union. In those moments, during which Tete would order me into positions that good taste and decency prevent me from describing, I would lose control of myself. I would fart, dribble, groan or even – at least on one occasion – bark loudly. Tete did not get pregnant; she knew her safe days and other tricks. I never saw any aspirins in her handbag.

I had always been a solitary person. I had always thought of myself as an outcast. Tete wanted to break this. Whenever there was a party, she would take me along. Journalists, she said, had to be outgoing. In Henrique, journalism was not a profession in which people ferreted out and presented information; we just regurgitated what the authorities gave us. This depressed me. I wanted to influence people. I wanted to reveal to the people on the island things they did not know. I always hoped that one day my colleagues and I at *Luz* would operate as proper journalists and not just purveyors of official lies.

There was a Writers' Union in Henrique. A man called Costa Santamaria was the general secretary. He had had a couple of poems published in Portugal, which enabled him to attend several cultural events all around the world. He was a sort of cultural ambassador of Henrique. Whenever he met someone of any importance, he would hand out a business card printed in baroque letters that read: COSTA SANTAMARIA – POET AND CRITIC OF POETRY.

Tete and I were very close to Costa Santamaria. In the evenings we often went to his house, where he delighted in playing the part of a poet. He had a long beard, shaggy hair, and smoked a pipe.

Costa Santamaria was a good man, a tropical dreamer. True, sometimes, like most thinkers on the island, he had to fawn before the party, but he carried himself with dignity. He and Tete had founded a group that usually met on Thursday evenings to discuss all sorts of issues: the position of women in society; Marxism and development; traditional Henriquean culture. I had attended only three of these meetings. One thing that had struck me about them was that half of the audience would be ordinary Henriqueans in search of a good argument. The other half – some with hidden tape recorders – belonged to the SIS. The East Germans had taught them not to let anything the citizens said slip by. The East Germans had made two important contributions to Henrique. First, they helped build a gigantic brewery; this had made them very popular with Henriqueans, who could hardly imagine an existence without alcohol. Secondly, they helped create and maintain the secret police: there were drunken spies all over the island. I had often felt uneasy in those meetings because Tete spoke her mind. She was not afraid of the party. In the discussions, she would denounce party leaders as a corrupt lot who were oblivious to the direction the island was taking. Later, I discovered that the secret policemen had not reported most of her comments because they were just too bold: the authorities would have suspected that they were made up by secret-police people.

Tete was soon off to Portugal on a scholarship. For a whole year we communicated through letters. Hers were very moving. She said she had many dreams for Henrique. Some of her letters were extremely critical of the government. She said Marxism was not going to take Henriqueans anywhere. What Henrique needed were incentives for the people to produce more. Tete wrote about the need for democracy.

I missed Tete, mainly because in her absence I was not invited to the parties of the Monangolas. I was anxious for her to come back; I wanted to keep mingling with the people who mattered.

Tete returned from Europe a changed person. Her mind, which had always been broad, had become even broader. In Spain, Tete had gone to an opera in Madrid and been very impressed by what she had heard and seen. She got me to listen to *Cosí fan tutte*, *Le nozze di Figaro*, *Don Giovanni*. Whenever I played opera in my little house, I played it with the volume very low; I did not want my neighbours to think I was being lordly. It was only when I played African music that I turned the volume knob almost to the loudest point. We got so deep into opera that we even made love to it: the duet from *The Pearl Fishers* was our favourite. We timed it in such a way that we both climaxed when it came to an end. True, this was perhaps somewhat mechanical, but Tete never minded and I was willing to comply.

Several men asked me how I coped with Tete, a woman who held such strong views. I told them that I was a tough man. In a way, I felt that by sticking to Tete, by respecting her views, I was being decent. I felt very pure when I walked in the streets. The evil that Sister Aluveva had referred to when I had lied to my orphanage colleagues was something of the past. When Rito and I met these days we would both laugh at the incident. I regained the purity I must have had as a small child.

Tete irritated many people with her dissident and outspoken views. She was, however, very tender with me. Sometimes, she behaved as though she were my mother. I knew when to bring that out in her. All I had to do was to play my confused-motherless-little-boy act. One evening, we were in bed just fondling each other. I was lying on Tete's lap, like a baby. I was doing what I enjoyed best – sucking her left breast. In those minutes, Tete would look at me – a bearded man – the way she would have looked at an infant. Suddenly, she began to hum into my ears a song that reminded me of my childhood. I felt so loved.

I laughed and said, 'You won't believe this, but my mother used to like that song too.'

Tete said, 'All mothers and babies in Henrique love that song. I am now your mother.'

2

A Little History

I am writing this far away from the island of my birth. Everyone asks where Henrique is. Even people from São Tomé, that little island that has so much in common with us, often pretend not to know where Henrique is. Cape Verdeans, Angolans, Mozambicans are all baffled by this island although, in some ways, we are alike. After all, we all belong to the Portuguese-speaking world. We belong to those islands thrown into the armpit of Africa.

Many people do not know of Henrique, for it has never made it into the international headlines. Although there is a volcanic mountain near Diaz city, it has never erupted. Although we lacked many resources, we had some wealth such as seafood, bauxite, timber, cocoa, bananas and sugar. We have never had a famine. Occasionally, some Western tourists find themselves on our island. Nothing mesmerises them. Some tourists say that the most striking aspect of the island is the drunkenness of the people. For us

40

Henriqueans, our island is the world. Even now most of my compatriots can't imagine living elsewhere but on the island.

Henrique was – as our former colonial masters used to tell us – discovered by the Portuguese when Bartholomeu Diaz was on his way to India. Some historians maintain that it was Bartholomeu Diaz himself who discovered the island. Others maintain that it was a group of sailors who were with him. This detail has sparked off much debate. Everyone agrees, however, that sometime at the beginning of the last century, Portuguese landowners started planting cocoa on the island. The landowners brought workers from the mainland to work on the plantations. Some Henriqueans can trace their ancestry as far back as to the Sudan.

Henrique looks almost rectangular on most maps. At one end of the island is Diaz city, the capital, and its palatial mansions at Castelo, overlooking the sea. Cocoa plantations take up most of the island. The main road has now been tarred, thanks to Romanian aid; I do not know what Henrique had to pay in return for this favour. The road leads to Alves, the city with the best beaches. In the middle of the island are volcanic mountains that lead to sugar-cane plantations. At the other end of the island is Pololo, the main port. Next to Pololo are holiday camps built specially for East Germans. After helping Henriqueans to found the SIS, the East Germans retreated to the camps to enjoy the sea, the sun and evening barbecues; all amenities were available.

By African standards, Henrique – with a total

population of almost a hundred thousand – has modest resources. We have bananas, cocoa, timber and sugar to export, all of which belonged to Portuguese land-owners in the past. In 1975, when the Portuguese regime was overthrown, Henriquean nationalists, who had been operating from the Congo, returned to the island. They ordered the Portuguese to leave at once. The state took over the farms and proclaimed Henrique a Marxist state.

As I write in this exile that might turn out to be eternal, I wonder what was actually going on in Henrique. Did anyone ever ponder on the theories from abroad that people were taking to with such alacrity? Henriqueans lacked self-confidence: that is, both the rulers and their subjects. Those among the subjects who had been to school tried to prove their worth by mastering the official rhetoric. The rulers encouraged this opportunism and rewarded it in different ways.

Immediately after independence, people in Henrique could express their views, even people who had views that ran counter to those espoused by the party. There were people who went around Diaz city calling the president 'Chado' or 'Chadinho'. Everything was informal and relaxed. Soon, however, all citizens were required to refer to him as 'Comrade Doctor': after all, the president had been granted an honorary doctorate in politics from Patrice Lumumba University in Moscow. There were even those who disputed the official version of how the MHL had come to power. As soon as the coup in Portugal was announced, several political parties had sprung up on the island. These were all to be crushed out of existence. At *Luz*, we had specific instructions never to refer to these parties. Gradually, only the party's view in Henrique began to matter. As soon as the authorities proclaimed Marxism the national ideology, Eastern Europeans began to troop to the island, some on a break from their stint in Angola. Leonid Brezhnev, Fidel Castro, Erich Honecker, Nicolae Ceauşescu were among the world leaders who landed on Henrique. Every time one of these dignitaries came to our island there would be much joy. It was not, of course, that Henriqueans were actually pleased to see Honecker. There was joy because the main shops would suddenly fill up with food where there were usually many shortages. There would suddenly be more beer and dancing.

During these visits, most citizens of Diaz city went to the airport to sing praises to the president. *Luz* now referred to him as Comrade Doctor His Excellency President Machado Alves. A Soviet journalist, Ivan Semenov, wrote a long biography of President Alves tracing his revolutionary activities back to his childhood. The book maintained that the five-year-old future president had taken a trader to task for overcharging on toy soldiers. Mr Semenov had found countless people willing to give accounts of the amazing young Machado Alves. Not surprisingly, that book was a bestseller in Henrique: most people who could read had copies of it. I had three: one in the office and two at home. This book was soon followed by the collected works of Machado Alves, with an introduction by Costa Santamaria in which he said Machado Alves was indeed the Henriquean Lenin. Costa Santamaria predicted that it would not be long before the world would have to contend with Alvesism. Many Henriqueans believed Machado Alves to be a genius. It was the usual African disease – that obsession with the adulation of political leaders. I now suspect that it sprang from people's conviction that by praising leaders they were somehow elevating themselves. They believed that they somehow came to share the same qualities they were attributing to their leaders.

Tete hated that blind adulation of Machado Alves. She often whispered into my ears that her father had told her Machado in his youth had not been as illustrious as Mr Semenov wanted the world to believe. I told Tete to shut up, reminding her that the SIS was ruthless. In those days, we all feared the security people; they were, after all, everywhere. We could tell them apart from other Henriqueans because they all wore brown leather shoes. Also, they all wore gold bracelets and reeked of Old Spice after-shave. The security people thought of themselves as another race; they mixed very little, and occasionally swore in German. The East Germans had endowed them not only with torture techniques, but also with the proper vocabulary to express their most profane thoughts.

In short, Henrique was a little island off the west coast of Africa ruled by an élite very similar to the dictatorships on the mainland.

3

The Coup

At weekends, there were many parties in Diaz city. On one particular weekend, Tete and I had a choice of seven parties. Tete insisted on going to Costa Santamaria's because, she said, she wanted to meet an Angolan friend of his who had been on the island for a week. This was a sending-off party. I, on the other hand, wanted to go to Beto's because I knew that he, like myself, was obsessed with samba. Tete's wish prevailed, as always. Costa Santamaria's party was uneventful: it was the usual crowd that preferred talking to dancing. These were the intelligentsia of the island; each of them thought of himself as some great literary figure. But as people became progressively more drunk there was less talking and more dancing.

The dancing went on into the morning. Just then, we were disturbed by the sound of gunfire. It was as though hundreds of fireworks had descended on the island. Everyone remained still. I was very scared. I could not even begin to guess what was behind the shooting. I could not imagine who was shooting whom. Tete and her colleagues looked more relaxed; but they all bore serious expressions on their faces.

Tete came over to me and whispered, 'It's a coup; this is the end of Alves.'

I did not reply. Several women there wanted to rush to their homes where they had left young children. Costa Santamaria told them not to leave or they would be caught in the exchange of fire.

Then, by daylight, the shooting stopped. Costa Santamaria brought out the radio and switched it on. I remember very clearly the words that President Alves was saying: 'Comrades, we should thank our armed forces for the valiant way in which they have been able to suppress the lackeys of imperialism who have attempted to invade our island. These vile mercenaries – who have all been apprehended – were certainly not acting on their own; there are countless reactionaries in our midst who collaborated with them. All will be brought before a special court and given appropriate punishment. The revolution will not be stopped. Finally, I would like to thank members of the Henriquean armed forces, who have proved once again that nothing intimidates them in defending the motherland. Victory will be certain!'

The message was repeated over and over again on the radio. Everyone in the house became solemn. The Angolan poet began to complain that this would mean he could not go home. He began to swear. Otherwise, everyone was silent. We were discussing in whispers who the possible invaders of the island were.

Suddenly, the house was stormed by soldiers. One of them had a list on which Tete's name and Costa Santamaria's name figured.

Tete held on to me and said, 'I am not going. I don't know anything. I am innocent.'

One of the soldiers stepped forward and pulled her away from me. I was flabbergasted. I wished I could protect Tete, but I was too frightened.

Costa Santamaria did not resist; he stepped forward and said, 'Let's go.'

Tete was crying, saying, 'Nando, you must do something about this. I am innocent. I don't know anything. Why me?'

I was confused. Part of me wanted to rescue Tete, but another kept warning me that I too would be taken if I attempted to rescue her. Soon, I was overwhelmed by the need to preserve myself. Tete had suddenly ceased to exist; I wanted to survive.

The soldier who had been reading from the list said, 'Calm down, Teresa Sampaio, no one has accused you of anything. Everything will turn out to be fine.'

That was how Costa Santamaria and Tete Sampaio were taken away. We never saw them again. We all dispersed. The Angolan poet complained that had he known his visit to Henrique would result in such a shambles he would have remained behind.

I walked home feeling very confused. I knew that after Tete, I would be next. On my way, I saw that groups of people had gathered, with bewildered expressions on their faces. They were all discussing the coup. Now and then a loud wail could be heard coming from one end of Diaz city. Maybe it was a mother who had lost a son or a woman who had just become a widow; I could not tell. I was frightened: my legs felt weak; my heart was beating fast. I breathed in slowly to calm myself, but to no avail: the feeling that danger was at hand was so deep in me that it felt as though it was circulating along with my blood. I was desperate for a toilet; all the contents of my stomach from the previous night decided to desert me at once. I ran to a house and asked loudly if I could use their latrine. Nobody answered me: everyone was terrified. As I sat in the latrine, I convinced myself that I was going to die; that I was going to suffer the fate of those who had been referred to in the broadcast as reactionaries.

I resumed my walk home still frightened. There were now armed men all over the streets. Strangely, none of them said a word to me. Maybe I had nothing to fear after all, I thought. If Tete had been involved with the counter-revolutionaries, that was her own business; she had not told me anything. I also realised that although I was deeply in love with Tete, there had always been aspects of her that had made me uneasy: complacency, arrogance, and other traits so typical of people from her clan. And, besides, I had always hated the Monangola clan. During the colonial days, they had been the people who did the clerical jobs: they had perceived themselves to be only a little below the plantation owners. Most of the island's dissidents – exiled in Portugal and elsewhere – belonged to the Monangola clan. When they talked of democracy, they meant that their voice should be heard. They did not care whether those whose forebears had toiled in the cocoa and coffee plantations were heard. The Monangolas twisted everything to fit their appetite for glory. Every revolt on the island, we are now told, had been masterminded by a Monangola; all the great things had been the work of a Monangola. I knew that this coup attempt just meant that one section of the Monangola clan had been trying to topple the other. Those of us who did not belong to their clan mattered little.

I decided at once to present myself to the police. I wanted to state in very clear terms that although I had been seeing Tete, and that I had made love to her, I had always been suspicious of her liaisons with Costa Santamaria. I intended to inform the police that I had always suspected Costa Santamaria of being in contact with members of the opposition during his many trips abroad.

The police headquarters were in the city centre, next to the cathedral. There were countless armed men when I got there. They all eyed me suspiciously (at least so I thought), but they let me through without posing any questions. The police station had previously been a hotel. There were several people seated in the foyer. I said who I was and that I wanted to see the police chief, a man called Kiki Alves (a close relation of the president) whom I knew well. Although he was slightly older than me, I recall a time when he had been the best basket-ball player on the island. I was ushered into Kiki's office by a dour man.

Kiki was on his walkie-talkie, sweating. He put down the walkie-talkie when he saw me and said, 'I have been expecting you, Nando.'

'I guessed so,' I replied.

Kiki sighed. 'She will be fine. We just need to get to the truth – the core of everything.'

I said, 'Comrade Chief, I will be frank. Although I was close to Tete, our political views never coincided. Teresa Sampaio has always been a reactionary. She used to say the most outrageous things about the president and the party. One day, she even said that Henrique did not have a future.'

Kiki picked up the walkie-talkie and intoned some words into it. Soon, a tall, stout man – whom I had always taken to be a medical assistant at the hospital – came into the office. He bade me follow him.

Kiki said, 'Tell him everything you have to say and then we will continue our conversation.'

The tall man was called Evaristo Davide. I was shocked when I realised that he too had an office at the police headquarters.

Evaristo banged the table and said, 'Fernando Luis, we've just sent a group to your house. I think you are in serious trouble. If you tell us the truth, you might just be able to survive – twenty years' imprisonment or so. I am telling you all this because I knew your mother; and, for that matter, your father.'

I was confused. I could think of nothing to say. My mind went completely blank. I felt very thirsty. As I write this, I cannot help despising myself; I cannot help thinking how cowardly I was. I was, of course, innocent: I had known nothing about the invasion; yet I felt as though I had been part of it. Evaristo passed me a cigarette. I shook my head.

Evaristo continued: 'What a relief that these invaders have failed! Imagine what it would have been like if they had managed to oust President Alves. Henrique would have vanished out of history at once.'

I said, 'Comrade Evaristo, I don't know anything.'

'Of course, you do not know everything; the whole operation must have been planned abroad. You and your colleagues are just the hapless victims of the machinations. You are mere cogs in the machinery. Now, tell me everything you know about Tete.'

'And Costa Santamaria,' I added.

'Good. Tell me everything; and, perhaps – and just perhaps – you might come out of this lightly.'

Evaristo switched on a portable tape recorder. I told him about all the comments Tete had made that had led me to believe she was opposed to the government. I confess now that I exaggerated. Fear, that powerful demon, had seized me and I was prepared to say anything that might save me. In those minutes, I was thinking just of myself.

'Where is Tete?' I asked.

'There will be a trial. She is awaiting trial,' Evaristo replied.

I was led back to Kiki's office. He was now smiling and began to tell me at once how the invasion had been thwarted. The invaders, he said, had used two boats. They had been spotted by some fishermen out at sea. The security forces advanced at the invaders and a heated exchange had occurred.

'They are all with us,' Kiki said, 'and they have revealed everything.'

Kiki said, 'Fernando Luis, you should not let yourself be caught up in this. If you see clearly, everyone who was involved in this invasion has, in one way or another, connections with the Monangola clan. I am also a member of this clan; but I should confess to you that my grandmother worked in the plantations. Many of us Monangolas have been working hard to make sure that people like you – of humble origins – come to share power. The Monangolas are a petty-bourgeois clique; it is people like you who can save this island. That is why you, Fernando Luis, will have to cooperate with us. We are here to save you.'

The expression on Kiki's face was earnest. I believed every word he said. At least, I wanted to believe him. I said if there was an aspect of Tete I despised most, it was her belief that the Monangolas were intrinsically superior to all the other clans on the island. As I delivered myself of my views about Tete, Kiki kept nodding and making notes.

Evaristo came into the room and said, 'Fernando Luis, after due consideration, we are of the opinion that you might not be as innocent as you claim. If you are such a conscientious citizen, why did you not report Tete before? Why did you have to wait until this day?'

Kiki said, 'Evaristo, that is not fair. Maybe the actual significance of what Tete has been up to only gained meaning now, after the invasion.'

I nodded in agreement.

The interrogation continued for most of the day. There were, however, intervals when I was permitted to rest. During that time, I was led to a cell with one bed; a lavatory bowl was beside the bed. It was the most despicable room I had ever been in. As I write this, I question the logic that impelled men on our island to think of constructing cells like the one I was forced to be in, when there was a threat that diseases that had once been all but eradicated – such as malaria and sleeping sickness – were about to make a comeback. As I sat on the bed, I felt afraid. I imagined I would spend the rest of my life in that cell; but Evaristo did come for me and we continued with the thorny question of Tete's loyalty to the government.

I was released at last.

When I got home, there was a note from Diego Reis. He said I was needed at the newspaper at once. I guessed he had been looking for me to know whether I had been arrested. I borrowed my neighbour's bicycle and rushed to the paper. Everyone was there: a special edition to commemorate the thwarting of the invasion was being prepared. Diego Reis asked me to start writing the editorial, which was to go on the front page. In the meantime, all the institutions on the island were sending long messages congratulating the armed forces on having defeated the invaders, and expressing their support for President Alves. Not to have passed on the messages would have seemed an act of betrayal; even individuals had come to the newspaper to have their views written down.

I went to Diego and said, 'What should I write?'

Diego bared his teeth. 'A journalist not knowing what he should write at such times as these? Come on, get on with the editorial. You should call for the crushing of all those who had dealings with the invaders.'

I sat before the typewriter, unable to write a word. Then, suddenly, words began to flow:

THE MOMENT OF TRUTH

Yesterday, our valiant forces proved once again that they will not be cowed by the imperialists. Under the guidance of our most beloved president, Machado Alves, the Henriquean people have affirmed once again not only their determination to remain free but also their ardent desire to keep the banner of the Socialist revolution aloft. Alas, the imperialists were not acting on their own; they had local agents who were well entrenched among the law-abiding and peace-loving citizens of the island. No mercy must be shown to these agents. Those who sow discordance among the people will reap their wrath. In the next days, as we have been told, the trials will begin. Henriqueans will have to be vigilant, for some of the agents of imperialism might try to work things in their favour through sophisticated arguments. The truth is that nothing short of death sentences will satisfy us. The people have been offended and justice must be done.

I wrote about the glorious history of the Henriquean people under the guidance of President Alves; and about the possible chaos had the imperialists come to power. The editorial ran to seven pages. I took them to Diego Reis, who sent them with a messenger to the minister of information. As we awaited the reply, I sat at my typewriter wondering how things would have been had the invasion proved to be successful. Yes, I would have had to write another editorial about how corrupt, incompetent and vulgar the Alves regime had been. I would have been delighted to have been associated with Tete. I would even have claimed to have had previous contact with the invaders; but – as I once heard an English woman say on the radio – treason never succeeds, because if it does it ceases to be so. I was taken up by my reverie when someone shook me. It was Diego.

He said, 'The minister says this is first-class journalism. He wants to meet you this evening. You go home to have a rest; someone will be coming for you in the evening.'

I rode the bicycle back home. Surprisingly, it was as though nothing had happened in Henrique: the women were busy cooking; the men were busy gathering in small groups to drink and to play cards. I even remember overhearing an argument over football.

Everything seemed to have happened so fast. From the morning the armed men had stormed the party to that evening, it was as though the world had changed. However hard I tried, the thought of Tete kept forcing itself into my mind. I imagined her alone in a cell, cursing me. I imagined her crying.

I had a bath and tried to sleep. I am, by nature, a very light sleeper; the crying of a baby nearby can awaken me. As I was trying to sleep, I heard myself mutter a prayer. This surprised me: I had always thought of myself as an atheist.

In the evening, I got ready and waited for the man from the ministry of information. At eight-thirty sharp, a black Mercedes stopped in front of my house and I heard a knock on the door. The minister of information was a lean, tall, bearded man called Jesse Torres. It was said he had become an acquaintance of the president during their high-school days. The most intrepid even maintained that Jesse Torres used to write President Alves's homework.

The rhetoric was that Henrique would one day become a socialist state; a state of perfect equality. This goal had not yet been attained; hence some slightly disconcerting aspects to the country such as the opulence in which the ministers lived. When the Portuguese left, their large houses were handed over to the government ministers. The ministers, like the Portuguese landowners, could not conceive of life on the island without maids, servants, cooks and gardeners. Women who had been living in the poorer quarters of Diaz city suddenly forgot how to cook or to make beds, like the wives of the Portuguese colonials. Jesse Torres was one of the many men who had been married in exile to – as it was said – an unattractive rural woman. As soon as he became a minister, Jesse Torres decided to find a better wife, Berta Pires, one of the finest belles of the Monangola clan. Not being articulate enough, these women of the struggle packed their few belongings and vanished into the many ghettos of Henrique, where they found men who did not mind the fact that they were more comfortable speaking patois than the refined Portuguese of the Monangolas.

There was a guard at the entrance of the house. I was led to the sitting-room by a charming maid, who said she had once worked at the orphanage. (I did not remember her.) In the background, I could hear children giggling as they watched a programme from some imperialist country on the video. I had never seen so much wealth in my life. It was as though I was not in Henrique. There were several photographs of President Alves on the wall; these were interspersed with photographs of the Torres family. At one end of the room stood a huge television set. Next to it was some hi-fi equipment with so many knobs it looked as though it could make music on its own. The chairs were all made of some white material. At one end of the room was a large desk that might have been made of mahogany. Soon, the maid came back and led me to another room. It was the office. Jesse Torres was on the telephone.

The maid left and Jesse Torres said, 'Please, sit down. Would you like a beer?'

'Yes, please,' I replied.

'Emaculada,' Jesse Torres shouted out, 'bring two beers! I mean canned beer, not that other awful stuff.' He turned to me and said, 'I don't like Henriquean beer. Do you?'

'Sometimes.'

'This is the problem with our socialist brothers; their products are so inferior. I mean, these East Germans came here and tried to force us to drink something no better than urine. I prefer South African beer.'

I did not know what to say to that. It was certainly a very bold statement, coming from the minister of information. In Henrique, there were some who could say what they thought; others had to measure their every word. I guessed that Jesse Torres made such an outrageous statement to show me just how powerful he was. I felt belittled before him.

Jesse Torres said, 'Now, to the main point: the editorial you wrote was excellent. The president has already read it and he says you are a very good journalist. But, Luis, the main reason I have called you here is that you have been proposed to join the vanguard of the revolution. From now on, you won't be a mere journalist. We want you also to do some work at Alpha Zulu camp.'

This frightened me even more. I had heard of Alpha Zulu camp – in the southern part of the island – as the place where those deemed to be political aberrants went to perish. I had always associated Alpha Zulu camp with torture. Some government critics had escaped from there and spoken to the major radio stations and had all maintained that Alpha Zulu was comparable to a concentration camp. Now, I had been asked to join this nefarious camp; to be part of the most despicable aspect of Henriquean life.

Jesse Torres said, 'All the members of the secret police have been discredited. They used their position to get themselves bottles of whisky and perfume for their women. It is time men who can guard the revolution came into the fold. I mean, reading that editorial, I realised at once that not only are you a loyal citizen but you know what it takes to be a proper citizen.'

He then said softly, 'Have you ever killed before?'

I shook my head slowly.

Jesse Torres smiled and said, 'Are you afraid of killing?'

I nodded slowly. I felt like a child. I had never expected to talk about death to the minister of information. I had expected to talk about propaganda, about articles. Jesse Torres suddenly began to seem different to me. His large hands, with long fingers, no longer impressed me. I was frightened and confused.

Holding me by the shoulder, Jesse Torres said, 'Either we save the revolution or we are all going to die.'

In that way, I became a member of the secret police, the SIS. I wrote many other editorials calling for vigilance and suchlike. I dreaded the day when I would have to kill. Fortunately, it seemed not to be coming. Meanwhile, I worked very hard at the newspaper. I was under the constant impression that someone out there was plotting to have me killed.

Tete and her collaborators were soon forgotten. There was no trial; they were all just shot dead. Although I met the security people almost every day, I did not ask what had happened to her. One day, when I summoned up enough courage, I asked Jesse Torres where Tete was. His curt reply was: 'Dead.' I had remained silent; but I wondered how Tete had died.

Tete's father had tried to protest about his daughter's arrest; but a severe beating had brought him back into line. In Henrique, there was a limit to the influence of the Monangolas. Although they wielded power, there was a core élite among them who ensured that the rest of the clan conformed to their wishes. If any of the Monangolas deviated from the correct line, they were dealt with ruthlessly.

Soon, it was as though Tete had never existed. Ordinary Henriqueans went on with their lives as though there had never been any turmoil on the island. In the day, when they could, they went to work in the cocoa, coffee and banana plantations – all owned by the state. In the evenings, they drank themselves silly, danced and kept hoping for the next day. Seeing hundreds of drunken men and women, I often fantasised about going around with a whip and flogging them all. These were a mediocre people who deserved a mediocre president. Like President Alves, these people felt that

Henrique was paradise. They lacked ambition. Even then, I felt Henrique could be better; we could improve things. Of course, I kept all these thoughts to myself. I did not want to become a martyr for an undeserving people.

I had no affection for Henriquean women. Tete was the only exception; the rest could have vanished during a cholera epidemic and I would not have minded. The women on our island, for instance, procreated as though babies were valuable commodities. Girls as young as sixteen often became mothers, and, being very limited in intelligence and ability, they produced limited children. In that way, mediocrity reproduced itself. During the colonial days, children could be incorporated into the island's economy as soon as it was possible. True, most of the money went to Portugal to sustain the colonial system; but Henriqueans could hold on to a shred of dignity because they did, at least, produce something. But nowadays, these girls who were hardly able to bathe themselves properly were producing imbeciles whose sole role in life would be to consume. I was pleased when there was a bout of cholera on the island. The problem with Henriquean riff-raff was that they emulated Monangolas. Because they could afford it, the Monangolas had strings of children. These children were, however, assured of a school place, education abroad and eventually a cushy government job. So I did not mind Monangola women having many children because I believed in earnest that they were reproducing the most cultured, valuable segment of the society, the leaders. Left to the Monangolas, Henrique would certainly be better.

If Henriquean women irritated me, then the men really brought out the worst in me. Perhaps the most despicable trait they had was fathering innumerable babies. These men saw themselves as some kind of stallions. It was not unusual in a bar to hear a man boast of how many children he had sired. These were men who, as it was said, went about with their cocks in hand. They were incorrigible opportunists. There was, for instance, a time when all citizens were supposed to attend spontaneous public rallies. Some of these men refused to be spontaneous. However, when the authorities said the rallies would culminate in free beer, even the sickly were to be seen at the rallies. Whenever a leader from a socialist country came to the island, there were countless people at the airport after beer. I hated all these men. I was very pleased when AIDS, that incurable disease, settled on the island; my secret wish was that as many people as possible would die. Henrique was a festering island with festering people. The only exceptions were, of course, the Monangolas; if they vanished, then the whole civilisation of the island would go. That was the reason why a special hospital in Portugal had been built for the Henriquean élite – the Monangolas – so that those who were most capable of dealing with the IMF and the World Bank were preserved.

That was not all. The élite had special shops, and at

the time I thought there was nothing wrong with this. What was the point in giving milk to babies who would turn out to be drunkards, loafers, free-loaders and concubines? The milk had to be preserved for the thinkers, for the people who would put Henrique on the map of the world. I thought this was the plain logic of all viable countries. After all, even Angola, that country we then considered a monument to social justice, had an élite with the same privileges as the Monangolas.

After the invasion, several countries sent troops as a gesture of solidarity with the Alves regime. From tiny São Tomé there were sheepish troops who would not have recognised a bullet; boorish troops from Guinea Bissau; and brutish troops from Angola. The Angolans, like a people once used to being subjugated, were desperate to subjugate us Henriqueans. They had done that to the São Toméans. Some Angolans even referred to São Tomé as their overseas territory. The five hundred Angolan bodies were shaking with desire: they wanted beer and women. These were the cowards – men who had been privileged enough not to serve in the army; the men who had the connections; second-rate men guarding a second-rate micro-state.

Although I knew I was safe, and that my stature in Henriquean society was assured, I hated the Angolans and their horrible Portuguese accents. They were the most pretentious people I had come across. Just because they had oil they thought they could boss everyone around. They were vulgar and dirty. The sight of an Angolan prig was nauseating. Angolans always wanted to talk about things they knew so little about. One evening, I overheard a man argue with some Angolan soldier about Henriquean history. The Angolan was getting everything wrong, but he could insist that he possessed the truth because he had a Russian automatic rifle strapped to his back. The Angolan with the rifle actually happened to have come from that country's riff-raff. Sometimes I wished that some invaders would come just to kill off these Angolans and then leave. I hated the Angolans. I wished that their war would devour as many of them as possible. What had the oil and their wealth benefited them? Oil had deluded the Angolans. Great nations are made by those who create; those who can transform the world around them. Angola was filled with consumers – like the Henriquean riff-raff – whose sole role in life was imitating and never creating. Although the Monangolas were pretentious, they did, sometimes, come up with ideas. The Angolan soldiers also ate a lot. Whenever I was invited to a dinner where Angolans would be present, I was shocked at how many helpings they had. It was as though they had just wandered out of some famine-stricken land. They also had very poor table manners: they sucked their teeth and often tried to use their forks as toothpicks at the table.

4

Camp Alpha Zulu

Strangely, I began to pride myself on having been initiated into the SIS. I felt as though I had been shot into existence for the first time: I had begun to matter. After six years as a simple reporter at *Luz*, I had felt that nobody took me seriously. Now, the news of my additional activities would filter slowly to the rest of the island, and the name Fernando Luis would no longer be associated with sycophancy. And – to my immense pleasure – I was given a Mazda car, which had belonged to Costa Santamaria. After being given driving lessons, I drove to Camp Alpha Zulu almost every evening. It was a pleasant drive, especially as I always played my favourite samba tunes.

The director of the SIS was a shy man called Alberto Guedes. I only met him once. Alberto Guedes was said to have a file on practically every citizen on the island. It was rumoured that he was a half-brother of President Alves.

All those who deviated from the party line were

brought to Camp Alpha Zulu. It was a dreaded camp. I felt proud that I had been brought there. It was a sign that I was trusted by those who mattered. My first duty was to write down the confessions of the detainees. Sergio Fogueira, my immediate boss, told me that most of the interrogators in the camp were almost illiterate. I had, therefore, to be there when the detainees had been tormented to the point of volunteering the truth. I was reminded that President Alves himself often read the confessions, so I had to make them as literate as possible.

Camp Alpha Zulu consisted of several ugly concrete buildings surrounded by many trees. It looked like something that had been created in an immense hurry and by very angry people. There were three principal blocks: the first, second and the third block. There was a small camp hospital, next to the kitchen, and there was the interrogation chamber, which was also the administrative part of the prison. The directorate of the SIS tried to keep changing the warders so they would not become too close to the detainees.

During my first duties, all I had to do was sit back in the large room to which the detainees were brought after being beaten. All I had to do as they talked was to keep writing down whatever they were saying. There was, however, a need to corroborate what the detainees said. Before long, I discovered that they were changing their stories. I knew we could not send these reports to the SIS headquarters.

I listened to the groaning of men as they were tortured in the room next door. It was then that I realised the potential my new sideline would afford me. I could break men's bodies and minds; and use the information to advance my position in society. Because I lacked the background of those people who mattered on the island, I had to ingratiate myself with the authorities in one way or another. It occurred to me then that, although I had been made a member of the SIS, I was never invited to banquets with foreign dignitaries. Great ambitions are often fired by simple urges. I felt that there were many mediocre people at *Luz* who were invited to banquets and ceremonies while I had been left out.

Although the warders changed as they were rotated, they were all obsessed with one thing: football. If they were not talking about it then they were listening to match commentaries on the radio. One evening, when I went to the camp, I found a man who was even listening to a football commentary in German – a language I was certain he did not understand – on a shortwave radio; whenever there was a goal scored, he would bang the table and laugh.

I eventually got close to the detainees. There were so many of them. I had known some of the detainees in Diaz city, but others were complete strangers to me. Pain was so etched on the faces of most of them that it was sometimes hard to discern their age: there were some who looked old but could have been my own age. At twenty-four, I was relatively young to be at Camp

Alpha Zulu; but then in those days age was almost irrelevant. What mattered most was power.

I had not realised that such a small island as Henrique would produce so many political aberrants. They spent most of their time in a large bunker-like cell with huge iron-bar gates. There was a bucket at one end of the cell, which they used as a toilet. They took turns at emptying it. The cell gave off a horrible stench. Only people like those would have endured such treatment. I hated the sycophantic nature of the detainees: as soon as I would come into their view, they would all start smiling or putting on sheepish expressions as though I did not know that, given the opportunity, they would have eaten me alive. These were the worst human beings I had ever come across. Some of them had rotting teeth; others had suppurating wounds (acquired from beatings), and they went on living, hoping one day to take their revenge.

The first man I had to deal with was a fat referee called Domingos Rosa. He had been found in possession of a letter from some dissident who was living in Portugal. An allusion to the letter Domingos Rosa had made in a restaurant was overheard by an SIS agent. The following day there was a search of his house and the letter was found. It was suspected that Domingos Rosa's contact with the opposition went beyond the letter; I had the duty of worming it out of him. The other warders were dying to have a go at him, presumably because he had made some decisions on the playing-field they had not taken to and they wanted to settle scores. Domingos Rosa was, of course, a Monangola. He was not a man known for contriteness. He saw life as a perpetual game, with himself as the referee.

Unlike other detainees, who were tortured first before coming for interrogation, Domingos Rosa was brought straight to me. It had been assumed that the man would talk without being tortured. Interrogation usually started at three in the morning. When people are deprived of sleep, they are more likely to be honest. I was dressed in my military uniform; all SIS members were expected to wear military uniform when at Camp Alpha Zulu. I loved my American GI boots; I could not help looking at them as I paced about the interrogation room.

Domingos Rosa was very short, with a small neck, bulgy eyes and thick lips reddened by his love of wine. He had a harsh voice. We started off well. He apologised for the letter and swore that he would never dream of cooperating with anyone opposing the Alves regime. I kept on asking him questions.

Then, perhaps because he was beginning to relax, Domingos Rosa said in response to one of my questions, 'That is a stupid thing to say.'

I looked straight at him, not believing what I had heard. The two guards behind him were already salivating with eagerness; they wanted to start beating him. I got the guards to tie Domingos Rosa's arms around a huge log in the room. Then I got out a whip and began to lash him. This was the first such treatment I had ever meted out. Strangely, he did not cry.

The East Germans had been advising the SIS on how to operate. Unfortunately, I was not part of the group that had been trained by the East Germans. There is no need for special training in worming information out of people. Any man, given the chance, will discover for himself the best way of breaking people's bodies and minds.

I undressed Domingos Rosa; the sight of his flabby flesh made me nauseous and even more angry. He had a funny birthmark on his left buttock; it looked like a map of Italy. I continued lashing him on the buttocks. The man, who had been very quiet, began to moan; he squeezed the log hard, as though he were having intercourse with it, and began to bray. Among the things I learnt at Camp Alpha Zulu were the different cries men give out when in pain: some bray, others whimper, others bark, some even squeak. Domingos Rosa was braying; this giant of a man was crying out for his mother. The guards could not contain their laughter. As I lashed him, I saw his skin crackle, and raw flesh came into view; I continued lashing. I told one of the guards to bring me some salt, which he did promptly, to sprinkle on the split flesh. Domingos Rosa, the referee, lost control of himself: he urinated on the floor. It was the foamiest urine I had ever seen. We untied him and ordered him to swab the urine with his shirt. Domingos Rosa walked with difficulty; but he swabbed the urine, and, as he bent down to do it, he turned to the guards and said in a soft voice, 'Sorry about that.'

I did not see Domingos Rosa again for a week.

More detainees were brought; a couple of market women had reported that some men had been trying to recruit them for the opposition. These new inmates were from the suburbs of Diaz city. They were arrogant and self-confident in the first days after they arrived at Alpha Zulu camp; soon, however, they had been brought down to size.

One evening, there was a man called Ricardo who was suspected of being the head of the gang that had attempted to recruit market women. I wanted the truth from Ricardo, so I made an attempt to soften him up first. We put him on a table and tied him with ropes. We sealed his mouth with adhesive tape. I got some soldering wire, plugged it to the mains and started applying it to Ricardo's soles. He struggled, twitched and jerked, but the ropes held him tight. I kept applying the soldering wire to different places on his body; the room was filled with the powerful smell of burning flesh. I had not realised that human flesh was so fragile; it was almost like plastic. Ricardo had been twitching his mouth so much that the adhesive tape came off; the room was filled with the crying of this arrogant man. The guards applied more tape to his mouth. I turned the soldering wire to Ricardo's toenails, which I found to be immensely beautiful. My experience at Camp Alpha Zulu was that men had very bad-smelling feet. Ricardo was the only exception; his dainty little feet were so beautiful that burning them gave me a lot of pleasure. As I placed the soldering wire against his

71

nails, they went red with blood. We untied Ricardo and told him to walk off. He was in deep pain and kept giving out short, sharp cries of 'God! God! God!' I sent him to the cell; but ordered him back two hours later. He was still crying. There is something quite disconcerting in seeing a grown man crying. I usually avoided the eyes of my subjects (it weakens your resolve) but I glimpsed the look in Ricardo's eyes; they belied the sycophantic bearing of his body. There was defiance and determination in his eyes. I hated this. I wanted to kill that defiant look from his eyes; but I could think of no effective ways of doing so.

The reports I wrote about Domingos Rosa and Ricardo proved a success with the SIS directorate; they said they had been able to corroborate most of the things I had stated in the reports. I began to spend less time at *Luz*. Diego Reis, the editor, did not mind because he somehow felt that I would always write favourable reports about him to the SIS directorate. In fact, Diego Reis and the likes of him did not fall under my domain.

It was at this time that an inmate called Jaime Gato was brought to me. The message from Sergio Fogueira, my immediate boss, was that I had to extract as much as I could, at whatever cost. I imagined that I would be promoted at last if only I was careful in the way I worked Jaime Gato, who was a very tall, lean figure who worked in the customs department. I had known him previously when he had come to the orphanage to give us tennis lessons. Jaime Gato, it was suspected, was definitely a member of the opposition. In the search that had been carried out in his house, not only letters but magazines with items about opposition members had been found. After the original beating at the police station, Jaime admitted to harbouring anti-government sentiments. For me, this was a goldmine. I tortured Jaime Gato so much that in the end he was begging me to kill him. I did not.

One evening, as I strolled near the first block where the most valuable detainees were kept, I heard them singing some Christian song. I was the acting camp commander for a month because the actual commander had just gone on his annual holiday to Portugal, as did all high-ranking party officials. This was a very quick promotion for me; but then in the SIS people were promoted according to very different criteria than elsewhere. I ordered that no detainee in that block was to have any food until further notice – for singing without permission. Who did they think they were? Whenever they came to prison their first instinct was to play the role of martyrs. These were not principled people; they had supported the Alves regime when it had guaranteed them some privileges. If that same regime were to fall, they would switch their allegiance at once without thinking about it. These people deserved the treatment they received; a civilised people will receive civilised treatment; barbarians will receive barbaric treatment.

Although I have now left Henrique, and hope never to set foot there again, I intend to try to redeem myself.

I still believe that the people in Henrique did not deserve any better. Were they not, after all, the ones who went to chant for President Alves? Did they not all have Alves T-shirts? In fact, I think that without President Alves we would all have been nowhere; the world would never have heard of us. Those members of the opposition who kept passing pronouncements in Lisbon were simple opportunists. They did not know what was best for the people of Henrique; they wanted to sell the island to greedy foreigners. And these people who followed them – the ignorant ones – deserved the treatment they got. I ordered the guards not to give the detainees food for a week. I also ordered a thorough search of the cells to make sure there were no bits of food hidden.

The guards were delighted when I told them this. They would be able to take most of the camp food for themselves and sell it on the black market. During that week when the detainees had no food, there was much silence in the camp. When I went to their cells, I would find them lying down, deep in sleep. The human body amazes me; I have seen it pushed to the very limit. The men lost weight and looked weak after a week without food; but they were far from being dead. I wanted them to know that I was in charge. I ordered that each detainee could go to the kitchen, but on one condition: they had to crawl there. This, I calculated, would be the ultimate humiliation. And while in the dining area, I continued, they would have to eat without touching the food. The guards thought this was hilarious. In the evening during supper the detainees headed for the kitchen on all fours. This did not surprise me; there was no single person in the cells who deserved any respect. After all, they did not respect themselves. In the dining-hall, things went as I had instructed, the men were eating the cassava gruel with fish without using their hands. They all looked like pigs; one of them even started licking the plate. Some of the guards were having fun throwing biscuits about and having the men crawl after them. We also brought them water in a basin and made them drink from it like dogs. The guards told the detainees never to sing again or they would go without food and then again have to eat like the animals they were.

After that, things went back to normal and detainees were not expected to be down on all fours for most of the time. There was, however, one man called Ribeiro – he had worked as a truck driver in Angola – who continued crawling even when he was supposed to be upright. However hard the guards kicked him, Ribeiro insisted on going about on his hands and knees. I ordered them to bring him before me. They were going to drag him; but they said he smelled a lot. They kicked him and he crawled all the way to my office. The man looked like some pre-historic man – his beard had grown long and his eyes bulged. His mouth was drib-bling. As soon as he saw me he started to bark. This worried me a bit, because we could not dispense with this man; we had not interviewed him yet.

I said, 'Ribeiro Colomo, get back to your senses.'

He barked. He continued barking, and the guards started laughing, saying the man had really gone berserk. I looked into Ribeiro's eyes and knew very well that he was not mad. I heard in that barking a mockery of me and the system. This was a man enacting a parody; by pretending to be an animal, he was preserving his dignity. By barking, he had built a fence around himself, something we could not assail. Ribeiro had made the mistake many of them made of thinking that most of us in the SIS were dunces, like the rest of the guards. There were, in the SIS, people like myself whose minds went beyond the prosaic. I felt insulted.

I said, 'Ribeiro, you won't get away with this. I can read your mind.'

He continued barking. Ribeiro was a Monangola – that omnipotent clan. I could read in the bark that he was saying I was a rootless person who was selling his soul in a bid to advance in life. I could tell in his bark that he was calling me a bastard who had been rejected. This son of the most privileged clan on the island was getting back at me. I was not going to let him go on.

I stood up from my desk; and landed my boot in Ribeiro's stomach. He continued barking faintly. The guards drew back. I kicked him on the chest and felt something crack; he continued barking even louder. I could see blood oozing out from his bushy beard. He was still barking. I aimed my boot right into his face. Ribeiro stopped barking, stood up and knelt as though in prayer. This surprised me; I thought I had finished him off. The guards stood still. I aimed my boot straight into his stomach and felt it kick against his ribs. He fell down in complete silence. I gave his head the hardest kick I could master; the head became swollen at once. Ribeiro seemed to have fainted. I wanted to finish him off. I was not going to be insulted in that way. I turned him over (he smelt of sweat and dirt) and hit his face with the bottom of my boot. There was no reaction from him. I felt disappointed; I wanted some reaction from this Monangola. Either he was faking death or he was mocking me again, and in the presence of these guards. I rushed to my desk, pulled out a sharp army knife and slit his throat open. The whole body suddenly shot back to life. Blood began to spurt all over.

Unlike other people who cover the heads of their victims (the guards kept looking away), I kept looking at Ribeiro's face. I was not afraid of the dead; I was not afraid of death. I could only imagine my parents in coffins; and there was Tete, she had not even had a coffin. I cleaned the knife on Ribeiro's shirt and ordered the guards to take him out.

One of the guards said to me, 'Serves him right, he thought he was better than everyone else.'

I did not reply.

Ribeiro was wrapped in a blanket and buried near the banana plantation where prisoners were buried. I asked the guards to give me the exact location. A week after Ribeiro was buried, I was seized by the overwhelming desire to see his decomposing body. I had always wondered what really happened as the flesh peeled off. I had imagined my parents and Tete decomposing. One evening, when no one was in sight, I rushed with a shovel to the point where the guards said they had buried Ribeiro and began to dig. Soon, I came to the blanket. There was that heavy, sweet smell of decaying human flesh. Ribeiro's face looked greyish; it gave off a powerful smell. The flesh had not completely peeled off, but it looked like heavy make-up on which some rain had fallen; part of the beard seemed to have vanished. There was still that defiant look on his face; I spat on him, covered the blanket and buried him again. The grave was actually quite shallow. Before I left, I urinated on that Monangola's grave. Who did he think he was?

As I walked back to the camp, I found myself thinking of my mother. I felt lonely, but somehow happy. Before I had ever killed, I had always thought killing was something so monumentally evil that a man who had killed would never be able to live with himself in peace. This was patently false: the night after I had slit Ribeiro's throat open was the most peaceful I had ever had. After the killing, I felt a certain serenity descend on me. I had done something I had always wished to do, but which had always been denied to me. I felt fulfilled. I then felt that only those of us who had had the privilege of taking other people's lives knew the intense pleasure that went with slitting open a man's throat, cutting off life.

There was some other good news: the guards had reported Ribeiro's death (every detail of it), and my bosses were very pleased. In the SIS hierarchy, a man who had not taken a life was not to be trusted. I took the knife I had used to kill with and placed it in my lounge; it was so special for me.

After that, all the major cases were referred to me. There was the case of the Thick Fisherman, as I called him. He had questioned the party's right to tell him at what price to sell his catch. I had fun with him. He was so simple that I could read his mind with ease. I should have let him off quickly, but I kept him at Alpha Zulu hoping that some nugget would be wormed out of him. He confessed to all sorts of things. He even said that he had been meeting Rosa (the fabled mermaid in local lore) and that they had been plotting to overthrow the regime. Listening to him was real entertainment. Thick Fisherman, whose name was Armando, was related to some opposition leader who, it was said, was in Mozambique.

One Sunday afternoon, the guards had been listening to football commentary while I had been trying to read *Nostromo*. The guards were extremely put out when their favourite team lost. They were very edgy. It was then that cries were heard from the cells. The other detainees said Armando had fever and needed to be sent to the hospital wing. As the guards were leading Armando to the hospital wing, he asked for some water. The guards told him to wait. Then he called them savages. They brought him before me. He was trembling and very weak, his eyes were red.

Just then, the fisherman said, 'You will all burn in hell. Why do you treat a simple man like this? Independence has not given me anything.'

Again, I was not about to stand such abuse, and from a mere fisherman. Who did he think he was?

I said to the guards, 'Teach the bastard we are not here to joke! You can put him next to Ribeiro.'

The two guards threw Armando to the ground and kicked him until he fainted. They decided to wrap him in a blanket and bury him alive. When they went out to get the blanket, I hurried to finish him off. I actually quite liked the fisherman. Like me, he came from the lowly, unfortunate ones of Henrique. I felt the only service I could do for him was to finish him off so he would be dead when he was buried. I rushed up to him, squeezed his throat until I felt it break. When the guards came with the blanket, they felt his heart and were very disappointed to discover that he was already dead; they had been denied the pleasure of burying a live body.

There was also the case of the Indian; that was how I referred to him because he looked like an Indian. His grandfather, I later discovered, had come from Goa. He had straight black hair, and fine features. He had been brought to Alpha Zulu for insulting the president. I was still trying to get through the first chapters of *Nostromo* when I was disturbed by his cries. He was being beaten by a guard called Prato. I had then just acquired a new pistol. I walked over to the room, ordered everyone clear, aimed straight at the Indian's head, and pulled the trigger. There was a small hole on his forehead; but the force of the bullet had blasted the back of his head open. The Indian fell to the ground at once. Prato asked to have a go with the pistol. I let him have three shots; he aimed them at the Indian's stomach. After that, I continued with *Nostromo*, but could not understand a thing.

Among the many cases I dealt with I also remember that of Gregoria Luvas, the dandy said to have been having an affair with Nina Strasbourg. I had known him for a long time. He was very particular about his looks (he was quite handsome) and had fathered several children. His name was attached to many scandals on the island. There was, of course, the Nina Strasbourg scandal, which will never be forgotten on the island. Gregorio was a tailor. Some minister had ordered him to make a suit; but he, it was said, had preferred to give priority to some other customers. The minister did not have his suit even after three months. When the minister told Gregorio to watch out, Gregorio told him to fuck off. That was how he found himself at Alpha Zulu. Gregorio Luvas was a complete coward. When the guards tortured him for the first time, they had all fallen about with laughter: he had been wearing knickers. When the police had picked him up from the house of one of his several mistresses, he had mistaken her knickers for his underpants. I knew this girlfriend; she was called Fatima Almeida.

Gregorio was completely confused. There were people who came to Alpha Zulu and humiliated us (we had the final word most of the time); but there were others who were really hopeless. He often blubbered on about his innocence. Sometimes, he did, however, surprise me because he took punishment manfully. Gregorio was one of those who, as soon as they stepped into Alpha Zulu, convinced themselves that they were there to suffer. At first I pitied him; but later I realised that this was, after all, the man every girl in Henrique had wanted to go to bed with. He was lovable. One evening, I ordered him to be brought into the truth chamber, as we called it. I ordered the guards to undress Gregorio. He actually had a very beautiful body; everything about him seemed in proportion. He covered his penis with his hands.

I said, 'Gregorio Luvas, you were once the most popular man in Henrique. Let's see the erection which sent all the women wild.'

The guards started laughing.

Gregorio Luvas said, 'Fernando Luis, I am here to be beaten, or even killed. I am prepared for all the pain; but there is a point beyond which I can't go.'

'Come on,' I said, 'what has been seen by hundreds can be seen by three without much loss of dignity, if that's what you are going on about.'

'I value myself,' Gregorio Luvas said, looking at me with a look that seemed to suggest that I was corrupt, decadent and depraved.

Son of a bitch! Who did he think he was? Just because he had screwed so many women on the island did he think that he could humiliate me in front of the guards?

Gregorio Luvas was not a Monangola, but he mixed with them. When no person loved me in Henrique, there were hundreds of women who loved him. What was so special about him? Just because I was not lucky enough to have a beautiful body like his did not mean that I was worthless. And the bastard had insulted a minister. I vowed to teach him a lesson.

I said, 'There's much that you have not told us.' I turned to the guards: 'Come on, let's try the Ethiopia treatment.'

All the camps on the island had taken to the Ethiopia treatment. There was a bar that was suspended between two tall tables. Gregorio's hands were tied to his legs and we suspended him between the bar, facing down. We kept hitting him hard. The more I looked at his body, and just how beautiful it was, the more I felt like beating it to shreds. I hated him with all my heart. I felt like cutting off his penis (which was surprisingly small).

Gregorio kept crying and moaning. He kept saying he was sorry to the minister. He kept calling me 'brother'. Since when did I have a brother on the island? I kept hitting the soles of his feet. One of the guards brought a bucket filled with soapy water. We immersed Gregorio's head in it, and lifted it out when he began to struggle. We kept repeating it. While he was still in that position, I ordered one of the guards to bring the electrical equipment. Now I was going to give that penis – which had given so much pleasure to so many Monangola women – its final thrill. As soon as I applied the electricity, Gregorio cried out loudly and then fainted. We put him down on the floor and poured cold water over him.

As he lay there, I could not help admiring his body. How I wished that I could steal it from him and walk to the beach. I had bowed legs and spotty skin. In fact, at that time, I had just noticed that the skin of my testicles was peeling off after I had broken a pimple on it. Also, the uniform I wore was so coarse that it had caused some sores between my legs. I was very uncomfortable; and I envied everything about Gregorio. He had the finest pair of testicles I had ever seen. Seeing his naked body lying there in the pool of water was like seeing something I had always coveted but would never come to possess. Gregorio's body seemed to be defying me. It seemed to be saying to me that I was unlovable; that my body was mediocre. Gregorio had such a beautiful body; and yet he did not have to sweat to get it. He did not have to lie or kill or covet; nature had endowed him with it. I longed for it. I wished I could hide it somewhere and just look at it by myself. The feeling I had for that body is not the same as the one I felt when seeing a naked woman. Gregorio was just beautiful; and in that state, where I could do almost whatever I wanted to his body, he seemed even more beautiful. I was becoming mad with envy.

The guards were off drinking. They did their work better when drunk. I did not, however, need anything to get me going. Suddenly, I noticed that there were tears in my eyes. I longed for Gregorio's body, in the same way as some people long for beautiful cars. I rushed to one end of the truth chamber, picked up a panga and went for Gregorio's body.

The first stroke was to his head; the next was on his chest; the last on his lower torso. There was blood all over. Gregorio's body appeared even more beautiful as the blood filled the floor. I sat there looking at the body as the blood flowed out of it. No sight had ever moved me so much as that of Gregorio's body in the pool of blood. I wished I could stay there and look at it for ever. It was an amazing sight. The body kept defying me. It reminded me of my ugliness. It seemed to boast of the dozens of women who had caressed it; and the dozens of children it had created. I was mindful of the fact that it had perpetuated itself; and in that way it was going to last for ever, whereas I and my ugliness would be confined to where we belonged – the cesspit. The body spoke of beauty, and insisted that beauty was what was going to save Henrique and Africa. I felt isolated and unwanted.

The guards came back in, all psyched up. Each of them had a turn at Gregorio's body with the panga. The body was stuffed into a sack – which had previously contained rice – and buried near some banana field.

Two days after his death, I received an unsigned letter from Diaz city asking me to intervene with the authorities on behalf of Gregorio Luvas because he was my half-brother; he too had been fathered by Cabral Monteiro. I felt sick. I had tortured my own brother. I knew I was the very incarnation of the devil.

Soon, I was desperate to leave Camp Alpha Zulu. I hated the thought that the only distinction in life I could claim up till then was killing and torturing other people. I learnt a lot at Alpha Zulu camp. The human body is repulsive: a frightened man will urinate, even defecate without shame. I honestly failed to understand why some of those men wanted to live. Had I been in their position, I would surely have committed suicide. I also learnt how resistant the human spirit and body could be. I had seen men deprived of water and food and given the worst beatings, yet still refuse to be cowed.

Another reason I was eager to leave Camp Alpha Zulu was that I knew that some day the people of Henrique would come to know of my least pleasant deeds there. It occurred to me that I might one day be ashamed of my connections with the camp. The politicians who were benefiting from my work would be the very ones who would go on about the excesses and suchlike. I dreaded the thought of meeting some of the people I had tortured. I hated the thought of these people telling their children and families of the pain I was capable of inflicting. And I had hacked to death Gregorio Luvas, my own brother.

There were many times when I felt I needed to go somewhere to regain my innocence. But that was certainly wishful thinking. Anyone who has killed knows that inflicting death is like virginity: you only lose it once. Once you have taken a human life, it does not matter how many other lives you take; you can only sink further. Sometimes, people imagine that those who delight in slitting open other people's throats are extra-terrestrial beings. This is false. Although I had always known that I was capable of much evil, I was shocked that I could actually enjoy gouging out the eyes of a man using a Parker fountain pen. I was shocked that I could enjoy burning those I was interrogating with cigarettes.

I was desperate for innocence. I wrote to my immediate boss at the SIS, Sergio Fogueira, insisting that I needed to do more work at *Luz*. I ceased going to Camp Alpha Zulu and spent more time at the *Luz* office. Diego Reis was pleased to see me back. He flattered me and kept saying I had a great future. My other colleagues at the paper tried as hard as they could to ingratiate themselves with me, hoping that I would insert positive comments in their files. I hated them all; they were all hypocrites. I was well aware that if for some reason the Alves regime were to fall – and I never ruled that out – these people would be the first to denounce me.

There was, however, one person on the paper for whom I had a soft spot. Her name was Jill.

5

Jill

One afternoon, I was seated before my typewriter hoping that I would be overtaken by a rush of inspiration. With the deadline now three hours away, I had not completed the leader for the weekend edition of *Luz*. There were several topics hovering in my mind: the importance of loyalty to the party; criticism of the Lisbon-based opponents of the government; the importance of vigilance in the Henriquean revolution.

It was while I was staring at the typewriter that my eye caught sight of Jill. She had a lean body, darkish eyes and long hair. She had been with *Luz* for three months. We were the only people on the editorial floor. As I was still unable to think of words to fill the blank page, I began to think of Jill. I clamoured for her. I fantasised about being loved by her as much as Tete had loved me. Unlike many girls in Diaz city, there were no stories about Jill: she did not have a boyfriend; she had never been seen drunk; she was, in short, exceptional. She had another quality that made her extremely desirable: she came from the Monangola clan. Ever since Tete's execution, I had come to convince myself that I was too good for any other girl but a Monangola. When I had been seeing Tete, I had known many Monangolas. Now that she was dead I felt as though I had somehow ceased to exist. Sometimes I wished I had been born a Monangola. Monangolas spoke Portuguese with their own accent and expressions; I emulated them. I wished I could have their self-confidence and arrogance. I was thrilled when some people, the trash, mistook me for a Monangola.

When I was drafted into the SIS I thought my standing on the island was bound to rise. Soon, I began to suspect that it had not. Sometimes, I even felt that as a member of the SIS I was thought of by most people as a hunting dog for the Monangolas: doing the barking and the chasing for the Monangolas, but without being given so much as the bones of the catch. I despised myself for being so rootless. With a Monangola by my side, I was certain that people would finally come to accept me as a bona fide member of that élite.

I was besotted with Jill. Unlike other Henriquean girls who used all sorts of smelly stuff to treat their hair, Jill had beautiful tresses. She had a dark skin and a flat nose. (For some reason, this nose has remained engraved in my memory as a question mark.) Although I was so desperate for Jill, I never told her; I made sure that she did not notice what I felt for her. I noted everything about her – especially her clothes. I noted the white dress patterned with red and green flowers; the jeans and the T-shirt inscribed on the front with the name of an American college. Sometimes, Jill came to work with her hair in braids to which special green and red beads had been attached.

Suddenly, words began to flow from me and I set about typing the leader. In no time, it was ready. I exhorted the Henriqueans – as I had done many times in the past – to rally behind the party and President Machado Alves. The repetition of the familiar message bored me. But I knew that in Henrique, words had a world of their own; they obeyed a logic of their own. Those who had mastered the right words held the key to many things. I often, however, had doubts about these words, but when I realised that intellectuals of international prominence had come to the island and professed themselves impressed with our system, I convinced myself that whatever doubts I had were misplaced.

As I walked towards the editor's office, I saw Jill typing away furiously. (She worked on the letters' page.) Diego Reis was, of course, away. I had many reservations about Diego, a hopeless alcoholic who was editor of the paper only because of his connections with the Monangola clan. I left the leader in his office and walked back to my desk. It was a very hot day. Although it was a large room, the editorial office felt very humid; the air-conditioning system had not been working for a long time.

I was looking down on my typewriter, thinking of possible topics for leaders, when I heard Jill say, 'Nando, can you help me with the spelling of *background*?'

I called out the spelling to her. As I shouted, our eyes met, and Jill smiled – a polite, innocuous smile.

The editorial floor was soon filled with other reporters. As usual, the men were having a heated exchange: the sports editor was insisting that Eusebio was a better footballer than Pele; the man from the sub-editing desk was saying this was complete nonsense. Both men had their supporters. Arguments kept flaring up. There was only one issue on which Henriqueans were unanimous: politics – that is, the party's word was final.

I was deep into a magazine article when Jill came asking about the spelling of another English word. This time, she wanted to know how to spell 'rhythm'; she had not been able to find it because she had been looking under 'ri'.

I said, 'Jill, why are you so interested in English?'

'Henrique is a very small place,' Jill replied, smiling; 'I hope to explore the world some day and English will come in handy.'

'What?' I interjected. 'I hope you don't intend to leave us behind.'

Jill giggled and said, 'Oh, no. It is only that since the Island Hotel was opened, and tourists started coming, I have been unable to converse with them properly. By the way, I'm told that you are the person on the island with the best command of English.'

'God save me! I know enough English to understand the news on the radio and Phil Collins songs.'

'Nando, could you possibly help me with this English lesson I am working on? I mean, it can be sometime this evening – that is, if you are free.'

'Do you mind coming to my place?'

'Of course not!'

'But I am a bachelor!'

'That is even better. It means that I won't get some jealous woman pouring hot cooking oil on me.' Jill strutted away to her desk, smiling.

I could not type anything. My mind was fixed on the time that evening when Jill would come to see me. I only hoped that Xila, my housemaid, had bothered to clean the house. Diego came into the office, completely drunk; he was haranguing the chief sub about an error on the sports page that had been noted by one of his drinking chums. No one talked back to Diego: his word was final. The chief sub remained silent as Diego told him he was a semi-literate imbecile.

I left the *Luz* offices earlier than I was supposed to. Not only was I too exhausted to help in the proof-reading, but I had to prepare myself for Jill's visit that evening. I had just realised that I did not have enough drinks in my house. I got into my Mazda and drove to the special shop for the SIS.

Luz was situated in Machado Alves Avenue, which runs through Diaz city. I drove to the end of the avenue where the special SIS shop was. At the entrance, I did not have to show my identity card. In fact, the guard smiled obsequiously as he let me through. I ordered three bottles of whisky, one of Cinzano and several cans of Budweiser. I also ordered salted peanuts (imported from America) and some tuna fish. I did not order any other food because I had enough at home.

I got back into the car and drove home. Machado Alves Avenue went through the shanty town that sprawled across the city centre. There were many people milling about. I hated going through these shanties; in fact, whenever I came to that part of the city I had to close the windows of my car because I was suddenly bombarded with smells I could not stand: rotting fish, sewage, tobacco and the smell of special brew which, for whatever reason, was referred to as SH 79. Someone later told me that it meant Henriquean Smirnoff, which was invented in 1979. Fortunately, this local brew was lethal: many drunks had perished from it.

After the shanties, I drove through an expanse of green turf, which was part of a large golf-course. President Alves, it was said, had been on an official visit to Zambia when he had seen President Kaunda playing golf on television. From there on, a special golf-course was built on our island. Only dignitaries, of course, were allowed on it. The golf green stretched to the Castelo, the part of Diaz city where senior government officials lived. Theirs were impeccable mansions that the Portuguese had left behind. The governor's palace had a huge fence around it. It was now the official residence of the president.

I drove through Castelo at high speed. The police did not stop me at the many road-blocks: they knew who I was. When I arrived home, I was pleased to see that Xila had cleaned my bedroom and had also washed the bed sheets. The house was filled with the smell of some incense, which Xila, in her typical peasant way, said could ward off all evil spirits. Before I had started going to Camp Alpha Zulu, I would have bawled at Xila for burning the incense, but now I even encouraged her: I often imagined that there were many spirits out there braying for my life.

I was fond of Xila, but I had never felt attracted to her in a sexual way. Many single men on the island in a position similar to mine would have had a go at their maids at the first prompting from the devil. Xila gave off a very strong odour, which I found quite intimidating; it was not feminine at all. Xila lived with her mother, but now and then she spent the night with her current lover in a room that was attached to my house. I had originally intended to use that room as my office, but Xila had put a mattress there and she kept it very clean. I often sneaked into it in Xila's absence and invariably found flowers and incense next to the mattress. Xila had several lovers; I could not keep track of them. All I knew was that Xila and her lovers were in the habit of making love and having fights. Being an insomniac, I could hear practically all the sounds in my neighbourhood after midnight when everyone had gone to bed. I could hear the splashing of the waves or the singing of the birds. When Xila and her lovers had sex, I could hear them both groaning to a climax. As I listened to them, my imagination satisfying the voyeur in me, the image of Tete often came to my mind. Sometimes, after a bout of love-making, the lovers would start fighting. Xila never called out for help, despite the swollen lips or bruises she would have the following morning.

Jill lived near me. All civil servants of middling standing lived in my area. Jill's father was the head-master of the only high school on the island. It was, naturally, called the Machado Alves High School.

I took a chicken out of the fridge and soaked it with lemons. I liked it that way. Television had just been introduced on the island, and most people were glued to their sets during the evenings. They watched every-thing – from cartoons to long speeches by the presi-dent. Like most people who mattered on the island, I had a little black and white set. I hated television. True, the Brazilian soap operas gave many of us a glimpse into the other world. But that was all. I preferred to spend my evenings reading or listening to my short-wave radio.

At seven o'clock sharp, Jill arrived. Before she sat down she asked me to switch on my television set. The Brazilian soap opera that had most of the island enrap-tured was about to start. Xila and a dozen of her relatives – sons, nephews and suchlike – who did not have televisions came in with little stools to watch. Usually when the soap opera came on I would retire to my bedroom to follow radio broadcasts to Africa. One of the reasons why I hated watching this soap opera with Xila was that as it went on she would make comments about the characters, what they were wearing and where they fitted into the story. The soap opera was called *Os Sonhos da vida – The Dreams of Life*. It was about a poor girl, Ana, from the Brazilian interior, who comes to Rio de Janeiro to work as a maid. One night, she meets a man at a samba dance. It transpires that he is a wealthy aristocrat out slumming. The man, Alexandre Tomé, is bored with his wealth and falls for Ana. The two zoom around Rio in Alexandre Tomé's car. He showers her with jewels, which she refuses; love, she insists, cannot be bought. Then Alexandre Tomé is kidnapped; and it is Ana who comes to his rescue. There were several subplots in the story, which only Xila seemed to have mastered. The whole of Henrique came to a stop when this soap opera was on. Brazilian expressions began to filter into our Portuguese, to the horror of those Portuguese who came to visit the island. That was not all: women began to name their children after their favourite characters. Henrique was soon awash with Tomés, Anas, Invandros, Osvaldos. The island was soon obsessed with Brazil. People began to speak with Brazilian accents. When little children were asked what they wanted to be in the future they said they wanted to be like Alexandre

Tomé. Some young men even hoped to have the moustaches of some of the characters in the soap opera. Jill, Xila and her relatives were completely engrossed in the soap opera. I, however, remained fixed on Jill. I was in love with her.

As soon as *The Dreams of Life* came to the end, Xila and her relatives walked out, leaving the two of us to appreciate each other's company. Jill said she was too tired for the English lesson. She was dressed in the same clothes she had been wearing at the office, but I could tell that she had had a bath. She smelt of some special soap. As I rushed out to the kitchen to prepare the chicken, Jill remained in the lounge eyeing my bookshelf. I heard her say that her dream in life was to own as many books as I did.

She said, 'Some people have seen me come here. I know they will talk, but I don't care what they say.'

I did not reply, although that made me feel slightly nervous.

We ate the chicken and began to gossip about people on the island. Jill asked if I had enjoyed seeing *The Dreams of Life*. I asked Jill whether she wanted whisky or Cinzano; she said whisky. I poured her a glass and we began to discuss the merits of the English language over Portuguese. Well, we were not exactly discussing; I was holding forth about what made English such an outstanding language. I said English was the language with the largest vocabulary in the world; that there was practically no thought that could not be explained in

English. Jill was fascinated by all this. I kept pouring her more whisky. She became livelier. She smiled more.

I never drink when I am trying to seduce someone. Alcohol has the negative effect on me of making me silent and bringing unpleasant thoughts to my mind. I was seated beside Jill on the big sofa. She was helping herself to huge chunks of the chicken and going on about her father; she said he was a perfect case for a mental asylum. Then she went on about her school-mates; they sounded like a boring lot to me. In the meantime, I was dying to kiss Jill; the alcohol had made her lips seem so sensuous.

Plucking up courage, I said, 'Jill, I love you. I have always loved you.'

Jill burst out laughing. 'I know what you want. No way. I might be drunk, but I can still scream out loud. Nando, you're like a brother to me. No more nonsense about loving me.'

I had, by now, almost lost control of myself. The last woman I had kissed had been Tete. She it was who had fondled me. I was not desperate for sex; but I needed someone to fondle me. I needed someone who could love me. I was trying to fondle Jill's hair; she kept pushing my hand away.

I stood up and said to her, 'Follow me into the bedroom. I want to show you something very important.'

Jill said, 'Promise you won't get up to any funny tricks.'

'Of course I won't,' I replied.

In the bedroom, I pulled out the seven pistols I had beneath my mattress. I also showed her the knife I had used to slit so many throats open at Camp Alpha Zulu.

On seeing the pistols, Jill shrieked and said, 'Ah, I should have known. This might be the end of me.'

I smiled. I put away the pistols at once and we sat down on the bed.

Jill said, 'Nando, I really like you. I think you are very intelligent and you have a bright future.'

I held my arms around Jill and said, 'You have a very beautiful body. The best body in Henrique.'

Jill said, 'Thank you,' and she began to push me away. I forced her to lie on the bed. 'I'll scream,' she said, 'I'll scream!'

I was lying next to her. I said through my teeth, 'Let's make love.'

Jill chuckled and said, 'No way.'

We lay on the bed struggling with each other. I tried to fondle her breasts; she kept pulling my hand away. Then, as though in a dream, I found myself masturbating while lying on my back and holding on to Jill's hair. I was desperate for the smell of feminine hair. I had once taken that smell for granted; it had belonged to Tete. I closed my eyes as I masturbated. I imagined the sexiest women in Diaz city; but however hard I focused on these beauties, I could not come.

Then, the sight of a decomposing woman bearing all the looks of Teresa Sampaio came into my mind. I let go of Jill's hair. She looked on as I struggled to my peak. There was an expression of puzzlement and pity on

Jill's face. It was as though she were watching someone being tortured. She looked so shocked, she was unable to leave the room. But I was two years away from her; Tete's decomposing body was also about to climax. As I relieved myself on the decomposing body, I gave out a loud groan of pleasure.

Jill found the sight of a masturbating man so revolting that she vomited on me: bits of chicken and some yellowish liquid were suddenly heaped on my pubic hair. I stood up at once and rushed to the bathroom to wash myself clean. I hated myself. I had no dignity. I was not a real man. A woman had witnessed me abusing myself.

When I came back, Jill said, 'Sorry, Nando, but I had never seen that before. It really looks and smells horrible.'

I said, 'Sorry, Jill. I hope this incident will remain between just the two of us.'

'Of course it will, Nando.' Then, as though seized by some impulse, Jill bent over towards me and kissed me on the cheeks. She said, 'Nando, you are lonely. You will always be lonely. You know why?'

I shook my head and said, 'I don't. Please tell me why.'

'Ah, everyone on this island knows about you and Tete. I will be honest with you, Nando: people say you were happy to see her executed. You even wrote an article saying that everyone in her group should be smashed and crushed out of existence.'

I was fuming. 'Who on earth has been spreading half-truths about me?'

Jill said, 'Everybody knows that it was you who denounced Teresa to the authorities. Everyone knows that you owe your position in society to having betrayed someone who loved you.'

I said, 'You're drunk.'

Jill laughed and said, '*In vino veritas!*'

I wished I could strangle her. I hated her so much. She had confirmed what I had long been suspecting. I concluded that the reason she had refused to make love to me was because I did not belong to the Monangola clan. I missed Tete. She was the only Monangola who loved me for what I was.

We went back to the lounge, listened to some music in complete silence, then I drove Jill back home. On my way back, I continued feeling very wretched. I felt I could never come to find my innocence in Henrique. People would never come to forget my evil deeds. What pained me most was the thought that the Henriquean riff-raff – those people who spent most of their time drinking – would come to feel superior to me some day.

Two weeks after my meeting with Jill, I discovered that word had gone around the island that I had tried to make love to her, and that she had let me down. My advances to Jill, I learnt, had been discussed at several Henriquean dinners. I felt even more embarrassed when I walked in Diaz city.

Most Henriqueans spoke Portuguese using expressions that had been culled from Brazilian soap operas. This included most people from the Monangola clan. I decided to have a little go at them. It was a slight risk I was taking; but I summoned up all my courage to do it. It was my revenge against that daughter of the Monangolas who was now telling every other girl about my nasty little habit of coming on my own.

I wrote a leader advising Henriqueans to be careful when watching Brazilian soap operas. I said there was a myth spreading around the island – the myth that Brazil was a paradise of sorts. I wrote that this was a country where most of the wealth belonged to a tiny minority. I wrote that Brazil was actually despicable. To my surprise, the leader went down well with Diego Reis and William Torres. I was told that even President Machado was impressed by it. They did not want people to believe that there was any other country in the world better than Henrique. Also, the island's leaders had noted that the obsession people had with the Brazilian soap opera was unhealthy. It was even said that if the government were to order the soap opera to stop being shown there would be an uprising on the island. It was also said that many Henriqueans would have been prepared to die rather than be deprived of their favourite programme.

One evening, I could hardly believe it when William Torres informed me that it had been decided I should spend a month in Brazil to write about its ills. The articles were to centre on the theme that life was much better in Henrique. These articles, he continued, would destroy the myth of Brazil promoted by the soap operas. William Torres said most people took to the Brazilian soap operas because it added glamour to their lives. This in turn inflicted them with an intense sense of inferiority. My articles would be meant to boost the morale of most Henriqueans.

There was also another duty I had been ordered to carry out. As there were several members of the Henriquean opposition who had taken refuge in Brazil, I was to write a report on them for the SIS. I was given their addresses. However, as I prepared to leave for Brazil, I was overwhelmed by the hope that I would somehow rescue my depraved soul and regain some innocence.

6

The Flight Into Innocence

On the eve of my departure, William Torres gave me five thousand dollars for my expenses. I was to take a flight to Lisbon and then connect to Brazil. At the time I thought the money I had been given would last for ever. The plane was filled with Angolans going to Europe to shop or into exile. As the plane prepared to take off, I was seized with fear. I now find it hard to believe that I, a man who had been so close to death, could be so jealous of my life. As the engines revved up, I kept wondering what would happen if the plane were to crash into the sea. Suddenly, the plane was off and Henrique was reduced to dots of light; then the plane gained altitude and I could see nothing below.

We landed in Lisbon late at night. I was met by the SIS man there, a short man called Andre Ingles. We got a taxi and drove to the President Hotel in Avenida da Liberdade. The taxi driver, a lean mulatto, said he was from Angola. He said he had been a police chief in some rural town, but was making better money as a taxi driver. He did most of the talking during the trip. Andre Ingles told me that I would have to catch the flight to Rio the following evening. In the meantime, he hoped I would enjoy myself in Lisbon. He offered to take me around, but I insisted on discovering the city on my own.

The following morning, I tramped the streets aimlessly. Although Portugal had not seemed to me as fascinating as Brazil, I had always hoped to go there. As a child in Henrique, I had once had to declaim a poem about the Tagus. For us Henriqueans, Brazil was the land of glamour; Portugal was the land of culture. In Lisbon, I felt very strange, for I felt as though I had returned to my homeland. In some ways, Henrique was not very different from Lisbon: people who met each other for the first time behaved as though they had been acquaintances all their lives. What excited me most about Lisbon was that I was a complete stranger; I could invent myself: I was being born again. Also, for the first time, it mattered little whether I was a Monangola or not. In Portugal, I was a Henriquean, period. When I told taxi drivers that I was a journalist, they believed me, and I myself believed that I had never been engaged in anything nastier than misspelling the name of an important government official. In Lisbon, I was able to forget about Camp Alpha Zulu and the SIS.

I had a small map of Lisbon and the next day I told the taxi driver to drop me at Rossio, where people gathered in cafés to chat and loaf. While standing at Rossio, I might have been in some African country: there were so many black people. I walked to the Terreiro do Passo to watch the ferries on the Tagus. Everything in Lisbon seemed huge. In Henrique, I had been brought up to imagine that everything in the world was built on the scale of Henrique.

I spent the rest of the day discovering Portugal. I had lunch in a small restaurant near the Marques de Pombal monument. I was reading the magazine *Jeune Afrique* when a black woman seated on the next table leaned over to me and said, 'Excuse me, are you from Africa?'

'Yes,' I replied, 'I am from Henrique.'

'Ah, the small island next to São Tomé.'

'Good, not many people know that.'

'I know about it because there was a coup attempt two years ago or something. Anyway, I remember some people calling for the Pope to intervene with the government.'

I thought this was gold-dust for the SIS. This girl was certainly a Henriquean who was just putting on a Brazilian accent. She was very attractive; she had a slim body, a face with fine features, large dark eyes and very long hair.

'Move over to my table,' I said.

'If you don't mind.'

'Fernando Luis,' I introduced myself. 'What is your name?'

'Sayonara Lunn.'

'Christ, what a name! Is it from a soap opera?'

'No, it's from a film. I was born at a time when they were showing a Japanese film called *Sayonara* in Brazil. It was a very romantic film.'

'So you are Brazilian! I ask because the accent has become universal due to soap operas.'

'I am Bahian. I am from Salvador.'

'I am on my way to Brazil.'

'Can't be! What, are you going to stay or just for tourism?'

'I am a journalist.'

'Then you must definitely come to Bahia. I will be going home in two days, and I will meet you. You'll love Bahia.'

Sayonara de Aparecida Lunn – so she wrote in my notebook – gave me her address. She told me that she was a painter and that she had come to Portugal in search of inspiration. As we bade each other farewell, Sayonara hugged me and kissed my cheeks. It was the warmest kiss I had ever had. For that fleeting moment, I felt loved and needed. I felt worthy.

I met Andre Ingles before my departure. He gave me another list of Henriqueans I was supposed to ask for when I got to Brazil. I do not remember how long the flight to Rio de Janeiro lasted because I was taken up with so many thoughts. Before the flight, I promised myself that this time I would read *Nostromo* from cover to cover; but my head was filled with other thoughts. I wondered what my first articles on Brazil would be about. I was thinking of ways to save the little money I had. The passengers next to me – two Scandinavian girls – were serious-looking, and were reading their holiday guides for most of the flight. One of them asked me in English where I was from. I told her.

We landed at Rio airport in the morning. The weather was much like Henrique, humid. In Rio, I was met by an SIS man called Americo Alves – undoubtedly related to President Alves. Apart from being the SIS man, I also discovered that Americo was involved with a trading company. I was certain that the president too was involved with this company. The SIS was all over the world. As we drove to my hotel in Ipanema, Americo Alves was beside himself as he spoke about the wonders of Brazil. I was, however, mesmerised by the size of everything; here, even people seemed to be larger to me.

Americo Alves was fulminating against the Henriquean dissidents in Brazil. When he railed against them, it was as though he were seized with the same anger that had seized us when we dealt with the detainees at Camp Alpha Zulu. This made me uneasy because I was in Brazil to forget my past. I wanted to be renewed. I felt stained; I hoped to be bleached by the innocence that – I imagined – I was going to find in Brazil. Americo said the Henriquean dissidents had deluded themselves with the idea that they could transform Henrique into a little Switzerland. He said this was the worst form of madness and all those who believed in it must die. Henrique, he said, could only be run by a man like President Alves who had the stamina for confronting all the mavericks and drunks of the island. In a way I agreed with Americo. Henriqueans, as I have said before, were a people who deserved the government and treatment they got.

Among the dissidents in Brazil were some members of the Monangola clan. They tended to dominate everything. These Monangolas went on about democracy and human rights. What did democracy or human rights mean to Xila or the detainees of Camp Alpha Zulu?

Americo suggested that the first article on just how unpleasant Brazil was supposed to be should feature Rocinha, the largest *favela* in Rio and, Americo maintained, in Brazil. Rocinha, Americo insisted, was the best example that could be used to foil the glamour of Brazil which had spread through Henrique. My hotel room in Ipanema faced the sea: the water was very blue and there was a large grey mountain in the background. Americo left me to discover Rio on my own.

I sat for a while at the window of my hotel room and watched people on the sea. Brazilians struck me as being very at ease with themselves. There were grown men tramping the streets in their underpants. The sight of men who were not fully dressed made me very uneasy, reminding me of the bodies I had seen at Camp Alpha Zulu.

At about midday, I decided to have a walk along the beach. I must have struck the Brazilians as being a complete greenhorn because I was dressed very formally: grey trousers, striped shirt, leather shoes. Everyone else on the beach was in shorts and light casual shirts. For these Brazilians, the beach was not just a place to swim; it was a place for intense fun. There were groups of men gathered all over playing volley-ball, badminton, football. Others were out to show off their bodies. There was a mulatto standing in front of an ice-cream cart reading a newspaper. He was dressed in brief swimming-trunks. My eyes were fixed on him. I felt I had seen that body before. It was that of Gregorio Luvas – my own half-brother, whom I chopped to pieces.

I sat on a bench looking at the body. It was one of the most pleasant sights I had ever seen. I wished I could sit on the bench and keep looking at it for ever. That body, too, kept defying me. It kept reminding me of my ugliness.

I hated myself. I wished I could get out of my body and be new. I felt as though a demon dwelled in me; I wished to have him exorcised from my soul. It troubled me to think that I delighted in other people's pain. As I walked along the beach thinking about my life, I was coming to the firm conclusion that I had been born with the devil. I could never love, and I also felt unlovable.

Trying to forget my past, I took a bus and then walked to the main train station downtown. There were many people. I had not realised that Brazil was so multiracial. Sometimes it felt as though I had flown to some other African country. At the main market everything seemed to be on sale: records, biscuits, plates, kebabs. A man with a megaphone was calling people to come and buy the eye of some special fish from the

Amazon. He maintained that it was a cure for all ailments.

I was drawn to a crowd that had gathered around a boy who was lying on splinters of broken bottles. The boy was young and was dressed in only underpants. He looked bored and almost oblivious to the crowd around him. Next to him was a man who kept saying the splinters could not hurt the boy because of his magical potions. Most people were so impressed by the boy that they left some money by his side. The boy had a very fine body – not as beautiful as Gregorio Luvas, but a body I would certainly have wished to be torn to pieces. As I watched, I was consumed by a desire to see the splinters hurt him. I began to imagine his body filled with wounds and his face contorted with pain.

I left the market for my first SIS assignment. I was supposed to go to the Hotel São Jorge in Bairro de Fatima, to trace any Henriqueans around. My brief was that if I met any, I was supposed to pose as a dissident and have them reveal as much as they could to me. As I walked to Bairro de Fatima, the hatred I felt for myself intensified. Here I was in Brazil, a land where I could finally find my innocence; a land offering so much that could dissolve all the evil thoughts I had harboured in Henrique. I was longing to be a new man. Alas, this was hardly possible. As the Angolans say, home is in your soul. I longed to flee from this soul so filled with layer upon layer of the soot of hatred.

Finding Hotel São Jorge was not hard. Black Africans could always be distinguished with ease from black

Brazilians by the way they dressed. Africans tended to be very formally dressed, as though they were about to go to a party. Brazilians, on the other hand, were very relaxed. Bairro de Fatima was in an impoverished area of Rio: houses were cramped and the streets were littered with rubbish. I found a group of Angolans chatting in front of Hotel São Jorge. I joined them. Not surprisingly, they were all talking about Brazilian soap operas they had watched. One of them was saying that Angolans had named some of their markets – such as Rock Sonteiro – after Brazilian soap-opera characters.

It soon emerged that there were three Henriqueans in the group. I introduced myself to them and said I had come to Brazil to stay. The Henriqueans called me aside and invited me to the nearest restaurant: they were all hungry for news from home. Each of them kept mentioning names and I was expected to say whether they were well or not. I lied that most people were fine. The three Henriqueans were all Monangolas; it was they who got scholarships and eventually became dissidents. Had these three remained on the island, they would certainly have met me at Camp Alpha Zulu.

The three Henriqueans were called Bento Ramires, Leopoldo Santamaria (no relation to the poet) and João Rosa. I was eager to know what they made of life in Brazil, but they insisted on delivering themselves of their views on the future of our island. I was bored stiff, for I had heard these dreams being declaimed by detainees at Camp Alpha Zulu – that is, before the Ethiopia treatment. These countrymen of mine offered to accommodate me. They even said they could help me become an exile in Brazil. I felt embarrassed before them. Here I was, the worst product of Henrique, in the midst of those who had not yet lost the best qualities of our people. These Henriqueans seemed genuinely concerned for me. As I told them about their relatives, they seemed to trust me even more. They all insisted that the days of the Alves regime were numbered. They said Henrique would one day become the beacon of democracy and tolerance in Africa.

That evening, the three Henriqueans invited me to a discothèque called Help, somewhere in front of the beach near Avenida da Nossa Senhora. I wore my dancing uniform – shiny grey trousers and translucent yellow shirt – and hailed a taxi at the appointed time to take me to Help. This was the luxury I had all along been imagining: flashing lights, loud pop music – sometimes too monotonous – and pretty, vain girls. It dawned on me before long that Help was a haunt for sailors: all the girls there made a point of speaking English to any man. The three Henriqueans were soon on the floor, stomping to disco music. I preferred to sit by myself observing the dancers. Everyone here was out to show off. Some of the girls, who had the shapeliest bodies I had ever seen, made a point of dancing on a stage, to be seen by everyone. One girl was dancing before her image on a mirror. Even the men made a point of being seen.

Bento came up to me and said, 'What are you? A spy

or what? Come on, come and show us the latest steps from Diaz city.'

I strolled over to the floor and started dancing. It was like punishment. I only dance when I become enraptured by the rhythm; for me, dancing is like some religious ceremony. This kind of dancing, which seemed to me to be as routine as goose stepping, failed to move me. After a while Bento suggested we move to Columbus, another discothèque favoured by Angolans and Henriqueans. Leopoldo suggested that we walk over to some nearby *forro*. This, I was told, was a dance attended by the poor. These dances were as spirited as the dances in Henrique. To get to this *forro*, we had to walk along Copacabana. I could not believe it when Leopoldo told me that several of the people dressed as women were actually men who had acquired breasts and bouncy buttocks with the aid of special injections. João said that were it not for the high price he himself would have had a go at screwing one of those transvestites because they were often more attractive than women. The transvestites seemed to be mainly mulatto and white. I tried hard to discern the male feature in them: they all tended to have rough chins. But they were very friendly and one of them, a hefty fellow, even said, 'Do you want to have a little nap on Mummy's lap, sonny?' The other Henriqueans broke out laughing. Had I had the opportunity, I would certainly have had the nap; I was desperate for love.

My Henriquean countrymen felt superior to the transvestites. They insisted that homosexuality was one of the vices that would never be permitted to exist on our island. I agreed with them. I felt very superior; but a voice kept reminding me that the sins of the worst homosexual could not begin to compare to mine. It was one thing to screw other men; it was quite another to chop their bodies to pieces. There was no one on earth I could in fact be superior to. I was as depraved as humans could get.

We got to the *forro* at last. It was full. A band was playing and people were holding each other tight as they danced. João found me a partner, a lean Indian-looking girl who knew my fellow Henriqueans. I said to her above the music that I did not know how to dance to that music. She held me tight and taught me the steps. Soon, I was deep into the dance, which was quite athletic; I had to move with very quick steps, and I had to hold my partner tight. I tried to ask her name; but the music was too loud. This girl was certainly a bon viveur; she seemed to know every song and she sang along as the band played. I forgot all my sorrows, all my anxieties. I was suddenly catapulted into that world of ecstasy filled with innocence. The band played a slow, sentimental number (the singer was saying he would follow his lover all the way to heaven). The Indian girl laid her head on my shoulders as I drew her close. I felt her breasts press against my chest; I could tell she was not wearing a bra. As we danced, I wondered where her imagination had wandered to. Was she thinking of her lover? I wondered whether she would have continued in my hands if I told her what these hands were capable of doing. I smelt her hair; it was so different from Tete's hair. It smelt like the hair of a little baby. The dance came to an end and the Indian girl bid me farewell. That was it: she vanished into the night. My fellow Henriqueans also bid me farewell; they said they needed to get a taxi to take them to Botafogo where they lived.

I decided to walk to Ipanema. On the way, I met several transvestites. I walked all the way to the beach. It was a beautiful sight – the waves in the background, the light from the hotel. I was slightly drunk. A helicopter was hovering above the beach; I wondered what it was searching for. Something brought me to sobriety: a couple was kissing on the sand. I looked closer and noticed that they were both tramps. Their possessions lay beside them as they kissed. The smell coming from the two of them was nauseating; but the vision of two humans so deeply in love was very moving. I wished I could have taken the place of the man and been caressed by the woman – no matter how dirty she was, so long as she professed her love for me. I walked on to my hotel and slept. I dreamt of Sayonara, the painter I had met in Lisbon.

The next day I went to Rocinha, the infamous *favela*. I saw evidence of much squalor; but also of much joy. I had had a conversation with a black chambermaid who had advised me against going there; she said the place was filled with robbers and other social misfits. I insisted on going; she advised me to look as impoverished as possible. As I wandered through the slum, I saw all the evidence the Brazilians had excluded from their soap operas: naked children, tiny houses, immense poverty. I lost my way and when I asked a man with a surfboard to tell me where the bus-stop was he invited me to his house for coffee. He said he had never met a black person who spoke with an accent. The man was called Joe, and he lived in a tiny house, which had not only a fridge and a telephone but also a huge television set that was to be on for most of the time. Joe called several of his friends to come and meet me; then they took me to a white Angolan owner of a bakery, who was more than delighted to see me. The Angolan, whose name was Amaro, summoned his wife, a wiry Brazilian called Olinda, and introduced me to her. Olinda insisted on giving me coffee. Amaro was anxious to return to Angola as soon as the war was over. Olinda said she too hoped to go to Africa some day. I was moved by the warmth with which the people of Rocinha received me; I hoped to write about this in my article.

In Henrique, most people had been taught to treat all foreigners with suspicion; in fact, most people were encouraged to avoid them. Foreigners, went the party line, were out there to spy for the opposition. I had witnessed scenes in Henrique where people had fled from foreigners. In Brazil, I had suddenly found that which we seemed to be losing in Henrique. For all the squalor and poverty in Rocinha, there was still something we Henriqueans could learn from its people.

After a week in Rio, I found that I was unable to write my first article because, although there was so much that was negative, I was actually happy. When I walked in the streets nobody recognised me, and those thoughts – of wishing the worst to everyone – began to flash with less frequency in my mind. I made friends wherever I went. In cafés, the waiters asked me to talk about myself and Henrique. I reinvented myself, saying I was a mere journalist who hoped to write books one day. Camp Alpha Zulu never figured in my mind.

I began to feel that perhaps I had no future in Henrique. I wanted to dissolve into the Brazilian milieu and return home some day when people had forgotten about my deeds. It occurred to me that I could, perhaps, find myself a woman who would love me and bear me children. I would raise these children to respect other people and to learn how to love. I would lavish as much love as I could on my children. I found the prospect of having a family very exciting. There were other things I could do. I could, for instance, move right into the interior of Brazil and start my life afresh. I would even adopt a new name, and I would invent a new past for myself. It would not bother me if the offspring I was to have were never going to visit Henrique; after all, my roots there were so steeped in evil.

I decided to contact my fellow Henriqueans to ask them how I could become a refugee in Brazil. After all, they had offered to help me. I rang their Botafogo number from my hotel room.

'What do you want?' João barked out.

'I need to meet you soon,' I replied.

'You will meet us in your ass. We know all about you. We don't talk to SIS agents.' He hung up the telephone.

I felt lonely and dejected. I wished there was someone at hand I could share my sorrows with. I walked over to the beach and sat on a bench. I wished that my sorrows were contagious; I wished that all the happy people on the beach would feel as wretched as I did. I wished that the sea would cover me with a gigantic wave and take all my sins with it. I felt that even the unluckiest person on earth was more fortunate than myself. I felt that I carried all the burdens of the world on top of my head. I wanted to be a new man, but I could not because my home was in my soul. I was destined to die in sorrow.

The following day, Americo came to see me at the hotel. He had with him a letter from Henrique addressed to me. It was from Jill, asking me to buy her as many Machado de Assis novels as I could. At some point in the letter she wrote: 'I hope you are not too lonely.' Americo said he was still awaiting my report on the three Henriqueans. I said I would write it in a few days' time.

In the days that followed, I spent most of my time watching television (endless soap operas) and eating. I felt very tense. Sometimes I would go for very long walks or just sit on the beach and watch the waves till they transposed me to a world in which I was pure and lovable. There was so much in my mind I could not face, I had a constant struggle in pushing it to the very bottom of my soul. I felt like a man in need of some spiritual laxative. I began to feel there was only one way I could save myself from my sins: remaining in Brazil for the rest of my life.

One morning, I went to the hotel's reception, paid my bill and got a taxi. I was headed for the airport and my destination was Salvador. I felt that Bahia was my last salvation. The flight from Rio to Salvador lasted for three hours. I tried to read *Nostromo*, but I could not. I kept imagining Americo Alves's reaction on discovering that I had vanished from my hotel. I suspected that he would approach the police and report me as a missing person. I said to myself that I was going to report myself to the police as soon as I arrived in Salvador. I felt very lonely. I was wandering into the unknown. It occurred to me that there was also the possibility that the members of the SIS would be able to abduct me and have me transported to Henrique. They were, after all, everywhere. I dreaded being a detainee at Camp Alpha Zulu and facing the same slow, agonising death that I had inflicted on many people.

The plane landed, and I took a taxi to Salvador Praia Hotel where I had booked. As soon as I got into my room I rang Sayonara; she screamed with joy and told me to get a bus at once to see her. I boarded a bus going to Campo Grande and then changed for one that would stop at Pelourinho, where Sayonara lived. I had no clue where I was; I had to ask people, who were very willing to direct me to Rua Doutor Jose Joaquim. Sayonara's house was not hard to find.

Sayonara shrieked when she saw me; it was as

though I were a relative she had not seen for a long time. She ordered me to check out of the hotel as soon as possible. I said things were not that simple. I told her I intended to stay in Salvador.

'Oh, how beautiful!' she gasped. 'You won't be the first African who came to stay.'

Sayonara lived in a small house, which she had inherited from her mother. There was a lounge-cum-studio filled with canvases and some paintings. Sayonara was mainly interested in depicting scenes involving women: women cooking, women in a procession, women in a church. Then there was Sayonara's bedroom; all it had was a thin striped mattress on the floor and a huge radio-cassette recorder next to it. There was one other room and a kitchen.

'Won't your partner mind my presence?' I asked.

Sayonara laughed. 'Of course he won't; he just left me for a woman from Pau da Lima.'

I said, 'To tell you the truth, I am nervous about moving in here.'

'Stay in the hotel and spend a fortune if you want.'

That evening, Sayonara invited her friends and they took me to a samba session somewhere near Brotas. The five of us fitted into a small car and drove at a frightening speed to this small place where, I was told, some of the best samba in Salvador was playing. The driver was drunk and did not stop even when the traffic lights showed red. He defended his action by saying that many people had been attacked by robbers at traffic lights. Sayonara had changed into a brown skirt and white blouse; her colleagues were scantily clad. I was the only one who looked formal.

At this little place in Brotas I discovered that what we Henriqueans had been dancing was not samba. Sayonara started teaching me; I was too stiff to do it properly. Someone commented that she was teaching me the wrong samba – the samba of the *aficionados*. What I needed to be taught, he was saying, was the *samba burgues*, the bourgeois samba, which anyone could learn with ease. Sayonara shouted out that as an African I had to learn to dance to samba properly. Everyone began to look at us as Sayonara urged me to be light on my feet. She told me to imagine that I was sieving myself. I tried to imagine that, but I still could not do it right. The samba band consisted of four men playing little guitars and one man on the drums. Sayonara's friends kept buying drinks. After much effort, I picked up the rhythm. Sayonara kept telling me to imagine that I had stopped existing; that my body and the rhythm had become one and the same. I imagined that and, suddenly, everybody started clapping: I was doing the proper samba. The band played louder; and I wished the dance could go on for ever.

Sayonara's friends took turns at dancing with me. I felt so different when I realised that I was doing the samba as well as any Brazilian. I had changed. I was no longer the torturer of Camp Alpha Zulu, but the African who had learnt to samba as well as any Brazilian.

I discovered Salvador on my own. I wandered

through the streets of Barris, Federação, and sometimes wandered to Pau Miudo, Pau da Lima; and to
Liberdade, the quarter that reminded me of Africa
because it had so many black people. In the first week
that I was in Salvador, my samba improved to such a
point that I began to go to dances on my own. Sayonara
warned me to be slightly discriminating, but I went to
several places – Matatu, Cidade Nova, Retiro. The
wealthier part of Salvador did not interest me. I felt that
if I were to mix with the middle classes the SIS would
surely get hold of me. With the poor, the assertion that I
was an African who had decided to move to Salvador
did not elicit any further questions.

I did not know what to do next with my life. My
passion for samba seemed, however, to have saved me.
In samba, I had discovered the decent side to my soul. I
began to enjoy life, and I forgot about Camp Alpha
Zulu. Every night I sieved my body, it felt as though I
were rescuing myself from my past. I was sweating my
sins away. After every samba session I felt a new
person.

In the days, as I tramped aimlessly the streets of
Salvador, I often ended up at Campo Grande, where all
the buses came. Campo Grande was often filled with
the smell of palm oil because women dressed in the
traditional Bahian costume – white from head to foot –
were frying their wares in palm oil. I discovered that I
was actually drawn to the smell: it reminded me of
something very tender, but I could not remember what.
One day, while seated on a bench on Campo Grande,

the reason why palm oil meant so much to me explained itself. As a child, I had been used to my mother's habit of frying things in palm oil. The smell of palm oil brought me back to my mother's bosom. I do not know how reliable this explanation is, but I found it irresistible. I remember many things about my mother; I even remember the smell of her hair. Yes, the smell of palm oil took me to my mother's bosom. Sitting there in Campo Grande, I imagined myself being fondled by my mother. The smell of palm oil made me very happy.

At last I moved in to Sayonara's place. I slept in the spare room. For most of the day, before setting out in search of samba sessions, I would sit beside Sayonara as she worked. Sometimes, I sat by her, reading. She had many friends who were poets; I had to plough through their work to give her my reactions. Some of the poems were very profound; others almost incomprehensible, but I tried my best to understand them. I was desperate to get to *Nostromo*, but Sayonara kept shoving other books into my hands.

Sayonara was thirsty for ideas. She bought several newspapers every day; and she was the only Brazilian I had met who listened to shortwave radio. She tuned into the BBC Portuguese service to follow the events in Portuguese-speaking Africa. Although Sayonara was only two years my senior, I began to think of her as a wise old woman. In the evenings, the house was usually filled with her friends – girls who wanted a chat, Rastafarians in search of converts, curious people who had heard of the African staying with her. Until then, I realised that I had not noted just how different Brazilian Portuguese was from the Portuguese we spoke in Henrique. I had often heard Sayonara's friends exclaim, *'Ah, que tesão,'* which, in our Portuguese, could be translated as: 'Ah, what an erection!' But for Brazilian women it simply meant: 'Ah, what joy!' I had heard many of Sayonara's friends compliment her by saying, 'Baby, you are as good as a fuck.' I was, naturally, scandalised by this profanity; but for Sayonara's friends these expressions seemed innocuous.

On other days, Sayonara was so engrossed in her work she would not speak to me. During that time, she would play music by Milton Nascimento, whom she considered a genius, or Djavan Luz. When she was working on a solemn painting leaden with many meanings, Sayonara played Milton Nascimento; when she was painting something jovial, she played Djavan. On some occasions she would play Caetano Veloso or Gilberto Gil. There was much in the music of these singers that I admired, but to Sayonara they were like visionaries. Sometimes, she would replay a song ten times. This would almost drive me to insanity. Sayonara insisted, however, that she seemed to discover new layers with each replaying.

There was a man in the middle of Pelourinho – near the Jorge Amado museum – who, among other things, sold Sayonara's paintings. I never asked her how well she did. I enjoyed being in her presence. I enjoyed seeing her dreams and visions transposed to the canvas.

I bought most of the food and Sayonara did the cooking. She liked to fry most things in palm oil. Whenever the house was filled with the smell of palm oil, I felt completely happy. Sometimes we were both invited to some friend of Sayonara's. She seemed to know the whole city – perhaps this was not surprising since she had been born and raised there. She adored Salvador; to her, it was the best place on earth. She thought Pelourinho was the cultural capital of the world. This part of Salvador, with its old buildings, was always thriving with activities. In the evenings, there were several clubs booming out samba or some other music. In those days reggae was the rage, and everyone was listening to Bob Marley. Alpha Blondie, the Ivorian singer, had just released an album that had proved to be a big hit in Brazil.

Several people said they were eager to learn an African language; they were shocked to find out that, although I was fluent in Portuguese and English and had a reasonable command of French, I hardly spoke an African language, not even the Henriquean creole. When I told them that in countries such as Angola and Henrique the use of African languages among intellectuals was frowned upon, these Brazilians were shocked. While many people in Henrique who had seen *The Dreams of Life* dreamt of Brazil, Brazilians dreamt of Africa. Among many Salvadorean Blacks, for instance, African names were the vogue.

Every Thursday, people gathered in the Terreiro de Jesus after Mass to chat. This was a ritual that went back many years, I was told. Sayonara introduced me to her friends, who would ask after my family. At first this made me very uncomfortable; but I eventually found it easy because I had recreated my past, and it had now become true, even to myself. I could not imagine any other past for myself than the one I had invented.

I applied for political asylum – with Sayonara's help – and was soon recognised as a refugee in Brazil. I decided to try to get qualifications for university. I wanted to study Portuguese literature. Sayonara said she would help me get a job teaching English at some public school, and this would help me get through university. Sayonara was doing all this because she empathised with me. I began to think of her as a sister. I discovered that I had never been close to anyone. Still, I did not divulge my most intimate thoughts to her.

At this time, Sayonara had a crush on a lean man with dreadlocks who called himself Kongo. Kongo often came in the evenings to chat or to appreciate Sayonara's latest paintings. He played the bass guitar in some band. Sayonara made a point of going to every concert of his. She told me that there was something in Kongo she found irresistible; sometimes, she called him to come and see her. Kongo was, however, besotted with a girl from Massanraduba called Gina. Sayonara hoped that he would soon see sense and leave Gina.

Sayonara's last lover, Zeca, often came to visit her.

He was a tall man with a moustache who spoke very little. He was a medical assistant who – according to Sayonara – wrote poetry on the sly. She insisted that she loved Zeca, but he was in love with Helena, a nurse. I had to listen to Sayonara for long stretches of time complaining at the way Zeca had left her. Zeca was kind and polite. He invited me for dinner to his house; and one day, when we had met at some samba session, he bought me several beers and insisted that I join his table.

For a long time, I did not feel attracted to any woman, although there were so many around. I had lost all my sexual urges since I had begun rediscovering myself. I felt I was back in my infancy and convinced myself that I had to guard jealously the little innocence I had just engendered.

One evening, as Sayonara was cooking, I strolled over to the stove and felt myself being overwhelmed by a powerful emotion on seeing Sayonara. She looked so beautiful, wearing a light white dress with red and green patterns and with her hair worked into plaits. I felt like holding her, but I could not: I did not want to offend her. With the passing days, my love for Sayonara grew. I stopped going to samba sessions and spent more time with her. We had long discussions about almost anything that came to our minds. With Sayonara I learnt the pleasure of listening and being heard.

As my fondness for Sayonara increased, I began to imagine myself having a family with her. Looking at her beautiful eyes, I kept wondering whether our boys and girls would take after her or me. One afternoon, I realised that I had fallen in love with her.

That evening, I plucked up enough courage to say to Sayonara as we dined, 'You know that I love you.'

Sayonara stopped chewing. 'What a sense of timing! How can you tell me this when I am eating?'

'I couldn't contain myself.'

'I've been suspecting this for some time now. Thank you very much, Nando; but I don't think we are meant for each other.'

I did not know what to say.

Sayonara continued: 'I like you, Nando, very much. You're like a brother to me. If we were to bring passion into this, then our relationship wouldn't be so beautiful. Nando, it is nice to think that you are there for me; and I am here for you, not because we will end up in bed or anything like that, but because we enjoy each other's company.'

'I know what you're going on about,' I began, 'you're basing everything on this notion of love being some magical thing, affecting only those lucky enough to be in Cupid's path. Love is something that can be cultivated. I might not be the man of your dreams, Sayo, but my love for you has now become so strong, I can't think of my future without you. I often dream of having your beautiful fingers caress me.'

Sayonara shrieked and said, 'Love is dangerous, so complex, so wily! I've suffered in the past. I've learnt my lesson. I won't let myself fall in love with you. Nando, there'll be some other woman for you, not me.

Thank you very much for your love.'

I said nothing. Sayonara excused herself, saying she had to go to bed early. I sat on my own thinking about love. It pained me to realise that until then the only two women who had loved me were my mother and Teresa Sampaio. There were certainly many girls in Salvador with whom I could have had affairs, but these girls lacked what Sayonara had. For me, she had that something which she saw in Kongo, the bass player: something that cannot be explained. There was an instance when I felt very saddened. I wondered whether Sayonara had been told of my past at Camp Alpha Zulu. I wondered whether she too believed that I did not deserve to be loved.

One evening, while I was listening to the Radio France International news in English, Sayonara came into the lounge dressed in tight jeans and a white loose-fitting blouse. She was wearing blue sandals and a red beret that some Peruvian painter had given her. She sat beside me to tell me about the latest scandal: Dona Maria, our neighbour, was accusing her mother-in-law of trying to bewitch her. Sayonara had the strong smell of palm oil about her. I drew closer to her, and was overwhelmed by the smell. I craved to lie on her body and be fondled. As Sayonara rattled on about Dona Maria and her mother-in-law, I drew her close to me in one swoop and held her tight. Next thing, our tongues were wrestling with each other.

We stopped kissing and Sayonara said softly, 'Nando, this is not right.'

'I know,' I replied sheepishly, 'I'm sorry.'

Then our eyes met and this time Sayonara initiated the kissing. She was gentle and fondled my hair as she let the tip of her tongue explore my lips and then slide into my mouth. I gasped with pleasure. I felt like a baby. I felt loved. I felt needed. I opened her blouse and held her breasts; they felt soft and pure. Sayonara sat down on a mat. I bent over and began to suck the nipple of her left breast.

She kept sighing, 'Gently, gently, gently!'

We were about to continue exploring our bodies when a loud knock on the door forced us to stand up. We could not pretend there was no one in the house because the radio was on. Also, Sayonara seemed to be expecting someone. She buttoned her blouse quickly and went to the door. It was Kongo, the man of the bass guitar. He was going on about his girlfriend: she had threatened to leave him if he did not do away with his dreadlocks, which she detested. Sayonara comforted Kongo and said she would try to get Gina to learn to appreciate his dreadlocks. Throughout Kongo's presence Sayonara avoided looking straight at me.

As soon as Kongo left, Sayonara said, 'I hope that never happens again. Nando, remember that I'm not on the pill or anything; and some of these tricks can have hard consequences. I'm off to bed.'

I remained in the lounge. I was still seated there when Sayonara entered wearing a pink nightdress. I could see the outline of her white knickers beneath. She went to the toilet, then came back to sit beside me.

'What are you thinking?' she asked.

'Let's make love,' I said slowly.

'Is that all?' she asked.

'Yes.'

'Remember: gently, all the time gently. . . I am not made of rubber.'

I went over into Sayonara's bedroom. I had never really understood women's sexuality. Women had until then always struck me as mere tools for male pleasure. I had valued women for only one thing – love; yes, I valued them for that inexplicable thing. When I tried to switch off the lights, Sayonara told me to leave them on. As I was indulging in my favourite act – sucking her left breast – Sayonara asked me to sigh on them between the sucking.

As she lay there, Sayonara said softly, 'Imagine I was covered in honey; lick me clean gently.'

I obeyed her orders.

Then it was Sayonara's turn to caress me; she seemed to know every contour of my body, which flared on being touched. Then I clambered on her and we began to heave in unison. Her face soon contorted into an ugly mask of pleasure as she climaxed. I could not come, however hard I tried. Sayonara was very patient and told me to take it easy. I tried to imagine myself making love to Sayonara's friends. Still, I could not come. Sayonara seemed now completely exhausted. Then, the image of a decomposing woman bearing all the looks of Teresa Sampaio came into view. I came at once. I fell to Sayonara's side.

She said, 'I hope I don't get pregnant.'

I fell asleep and dreamt of Tete. In the dream, Tete was seated beside a coffin and kept asking why I had betrayed her.

When I awoke the next morning, Sayonara was not in the room. I found her in the lounge painting.

Two weeks later, both Sayonara and I were very anxious; we suspected that she was pregnant. Sayonara said that if she was, she would keep the baby because she did not believe in abortions. During that time, I often heard Sayonara talk to her friends about ways of procuring abortions. I was shocked by some of the methods they mentioned. It was said that a woman could bring on an early abortion by drinking a triple tot of whisky added to three spoons of salt dissolved in half a cup of water. There was also mention of extremely strong tea. There was mention of the red stems of cassava leaves, boiled and drunk. Others mentioned heavy, rough sex. I even heard of a girl who had just stuck her fingers in and pulled out the foetus. As I listened, I felt very frightened; I kept thinking of how my own mother had tried to get rid of me. Sayonara, on the other hand, kept saying she would never be able to forgive herself if she had an abortion. She believed that all women who aborted were plagued by misfortune for the rest of their lives. Sayonara said she had a serious dilemma because bearing the baby of a man whom she did not love was unfair to the baby. I kept asking her why she thought I was so unlovable.

'Nando,' Sayonara said one evening, 'you are

lovable, of course you are. It's just that you don't make me click. I know you can be very tender and understanding. I'm very proud of you and I really care for you. If I didn't care for you, I wouldn't have let you make love to me.'

Soon, there was immense relief in the house: Sayonara had her period. She was so overwhelmed with joy that she decided to give herself a treat and attend a concert near Campo Grande at which Kongo the bass guitarist was playing. I refused to go with her. Instead, I went to a samba party at Federação. The party was, as usual, lively. I was now doing the samba as perfectly as any Brazilian. A tall man was going around distributing paper roses and copies of his poems. The only thing about me that would have betrayed my foreignness was my accent. Some people imagined that I was from an English-speaking country, and they tried to practise their English on me. I danced for most of the night with Matilda – most people called her Tida – a girl I had met through Sayonara. Tida was an attractive, ambitious mulatta who aspired to become a millionaire some day. She made her living by baking cakes and selling them in the neighbourhood. Tida was obsessed with soul music, and whenever we met she made me translate Stevie Wonder's lyrics. It was through her that I discovered the angelic voice of Randy Crawford.

After the dance, I walked Tida home. Although most people said it was very unsafe to move around Salvador at night, I was convinced that nothing could intimidate me. Tida invited me into her home – two very tidy rooms at the back of a large house. There was a red sofa at one end of the sitting-room, a table on which some hi-fi equipment was perched. Next to it were a fridge and a stove, in which, I presumed, Tida baked her fabulous cakes. She put on a Randy Crawford tape. I wondered whether the neighbours would mind, since it was so late. She said they were away. Tida was an avid reader; there were several poetry books on a shelf next to the table. Salvadoreans adored poetry in the same way as they adored music.

Tida made me some very strong coffee. I hated strong coffee because I am an insomniac. I usually need all sorts of aids – physical fatigue, hot milk, herbs – to get to sleep. Tida was slightly younger than me (she must have been twenty-four), but as we chatted she often sounded like a very experienced woman, though she did not have the intelligence or curiosity of Sayonara. However, Tida was very modest about her limited abilities.

I asked her whether she was seeing someone. She said she had been going out with a young man from Liberdade who had suddenly converted to Islam: that is, the Chicago version of Islam brought to Salvador by black Americans. Tida said the man had demanded that she stopped attending samba parties and adopt a different lifestyle. Tida said she was a staunch Catholic and that if, for some reason, she were to convert to another religion then it would have to be *candomble* or *macumba*.

135

She said, 'Tell me, I'm really curious, are you having an affair with Sayonara?'

'Not at all,' I replied. 'Sayonara and I are just good friends. We have a very good relationship.'

'It's only that I've been hearing rumours. Well, the usual stories. Never mind.'

'Oh, Tida, nothing irritates me more than being teased. Tell me: what are people saying?'

'Well, I just got wind of the fact that Sayonara was worried about being pregnant. If there are some nibbles on the cheese, the first suspect is your local mouse. Have you guys been getting up to naughty games or what?'

'Well, it's one of those things. I'll be frank with you: Sayonara and I are about to fall in love.'

Tida said, 'Oh, some people are bloody lucky. Some of us are condemned to spinsterhood.'

She offered me another cup of coffee and we continued chatting. I stood up and said I was going to leave. Tida came to kiss me farewell on the cheeks; but I insisted on kissing her mouth. She closed her eyes and allowed me to slither my tongue into her mouth. I fondled her in the gentlest way that Sayonara could have wished. Tida was ready for me.

She said softly, 'Nando, please, I hope Sayonara won't get to know about this.'

'Of course she won't,' I replied.

I asked Tida whether she had any condoms. She said she had had some, but her mother – a Catholic fanatic to whom contraception was almost equal to murder – had discovered them when she had come to stay. The old woman had pricked the condoms with a needle in Tida's absence to make them ineffective.

While Sayonara valued gentleness throughout the act of love-making, Tida preferred it a bit rough. As I heaved on top of her, she breathed heavily and kept calling herself names. She called herself, among other things, a witch. It was as though I were not around. Tida, like Sayonara, insisted on having the lights on. I thought of Sayonara, but did not come; and then, the sight of a decomposing woman bearing Teresa Sampaio's looks came into view. I saw myself making love to Teresa Sampaio one beautiful evening by the beach. Tete had decomposed even further. As we rolled about in the sand, I kept begging for forgiveness. Tete groaned and shouted insults at Tida and Sayonara. We writhed in the sand until I came.

Tida, on the other hand, had not climaxed. She did, however, allow me to suck her left breast for a while. Before leaving, she offered me some special tea and a very tasty cake.

When I got home, I found Sayonara in the lounge reading a thick magazine.

As soon as I sat down, Sayonara frowned and said, 'You've been fucking someone. Who is it?'

I was lost for words.

Sayonara drew closer to me and said, 'Tell me! Who is it?'

'Tida.'

'I guessed so.'

'Why?'

'She's the only one who uses purple lipstick. See that mark on your shirt. Anyway, an experienced woman can easily tell a man who has been fucking.'

'I hope you don't mind.'

Sayonara threw the magazine to the floor. 'Yes, I mind,' she said. 'What do you take me for? Your whore or what?'

'But I thought you'd never come to love me,' I replied.

'Love is one thing, loyalty is another. I don't love you, but I am loyal to you. I have allowed myself to get very intimate with you, and I expect you to respect me. How would you feel if you discovered I'd been sleeping around with other men?'

'I'm sorry.'

'How can I face Tida now? I'm sure you tricked her into it; she's a decent person.'

Sayonara went to her room and shut the door. When I tried to knock on it she shouted out for me to leave her alone. I did not want to persist, fearing that the neighbours would hear our argument.

I went to bed. I had another dream: my mother came to me and gave me a bouquet of flowers, instructing me to hand them over to Sayonara. The following morning, I tried to talk to Sayonara, but she said she was too busy. I felt very uncomfortable; after all, I was living in her house. I thought of leaving. In the evening,

Sayonara bathed, put on her favourite clothes and went off to some party.

I felt very lonely and walked all the way to Campo Grande. I met Tida, who was on her way to a party given by a friend of hers. She asked me to accompany her. I liked dancing with Tida because she knew my steps. After the party, we got a taxi and drove to her house. We made love (Tete's decomposing body did the trick for me) and I walked back home.

I was expecting to be told to leave Sayonara's house at any moment. Although I had already made several friends in Salvador, I was not close to them. When we met, all we discussed was the weather; the forthcoming festivals (seemingly endless in Bahia); the situation in South Africa. Sometimes, there were heated political discussions. In Salvador, I often felt as though I had come to a newly independent country. Black nationalism was on the rise: Sayonara and her colleagues maintained that the type of history taught in Brazilian schools was biased against Africa. She complained that many black Brazilians knew next to nothing about African history, hence the formation of different carnival groupings that emphasised the African heritage. Some of Sayonara's friends invited me to their homes to talk about Africa. On those occasions, I felt very troubled. The Africa I represented was that of groans, of detention camps, of chains, of intolerance. I felt I was no different from those Africans of old who had colluded with the slave traders. Sayonara and her friends struck me as being better Africans; the splendour of the continent had survived the cargo ships, the plantations, humiliations and deprivations. With Sayonara, I felt I could pour out my soul to a sensitive spirit. Sayonara was the very incarnation of the innocence I craved.

I kept seeing Tida. Sometimes, when I was bored, I went to help her with her baking. She seemed to enjoy my company. Apparently, Tida and Sayonara had resolved their differences in what, I later learnt, was a tearful session of self-criticism. Sayonara criticised herself for copulating with a man she did not love; and Tida criticised herself for having allowed herself to be seduced. After that session, the two women kept talking to each other and promised each other that neither would ever make love with me again. I had given up on trying to get Sayonara to bed, but whenever I made any advances at Tida she told me to keep away.

Sayonara and I were reconciled. She said she hoped that I would forget everything. Sometimes I found myself at the same parties as both Sayonara and Tida.

One afternoon, I met Kongo of the bass guitar. He was in a restaurant with two friends. He asked me to join his table. His two friends left. Kongo offered to buy me a meal to celebrate his band's first recording.

As I ate, Kongo said, 'Hey, why have you been treating that jewel Sayonara so badly?'

I said, 'What has she said to you?'

'You broke the poor girl's heart. Why did you go off with that Tida?'

'How do you know about this?'

'I've known Sayonara for a long time. She always comes to weep on my shoulder. Some time ago, she came to see me and said you had disappointed her.'

'But Sayonara never loved me.'

'Any woman who allows a man to have a go without mentioning a price has a drop of love in her. What other proof of love would you like?'

'So you think Sayonara loves me?'

'Loves you? The woman thinks you have the key to paradise. Come on, you read books, you speak English and you have ideas. You've got a lot going for you.'

'Kongo, it's not as simple as that. I often wished I could play the guitar. It's you that Sayonara loves.'

'Rubbish, that's an old joke going back many years. Sayonara fancies you. Well, maybe because you are a foreigner you don't yet understand things; but Brazilian women express themselves in deeds, not words. Sayonara is just a little miffed with you. All you have to do is work at it and you'll have her in your arms again.'

That evening as I walked home I convinced myself that Sayonara did, perhaps, love me. If that was so, then I was very lucky. I had the previous day promised to pay Tida a visit, so I headed for her house. As she baked, we listened to Milton Nascimento. I got Tida to translate some of the lyrics because they were too Brazilian for me. Till then, I had been listening to samba, the music that made me forget my past, the music that seemed to purify me. Now, Tida was playing music that blew into my soul. Listening to Djavan, I was transposed to Henrique. It was a surprise to find

141

myself beginning to miss some aspects of the island.

I was overwhelmed by a very strange feeling. The island that I had so hated, the island I had always associated with backwardness, with narrowness, with sensuousness, had many things that were drawing me back to it. I had always thought of Henrique as hell itself. Brazil had seemed to me the place where I would exorcise my soul. I missed the water of our island streams. Brazilian water was tasteless; I had to add sugar when drinking it. The drunken men I had so much despised for having no ambition struck me now as being slightly quaint. I missed Diego Reis and his jokes. I wondered what had happened to Jill. She must be cursing me for having decided to defect and for not bringing her the Machado de Assis novels she had requested. I wondered who had moved into my house. I wondered where Xila and her relatives were now going to watch further happenings in *The Dreams of Life*. I imagined myself returning to Henrique some year when I had become an old man. My Brazilian spouse would accompany me. Yes, it would be Sayonara de Aparecida Lunn, her beauty still intact.

Tida shook me out of my reverie when she brought me dinner, fish with rice. I chatted on, and then Tida said there was something she had been longing to tell me: she had fallen in love with someone. As I walked home that evening, I decided to make fewer visits to Tida's house to avoid any friction with the man who made her click. I felt slightly jealous. Although I was not attracted to Tida, and I did not think much of her intellect, she was good company. There was a certain earthiness and honesty to her that I found very attractive.

It was very late when I left Tida's house. I was just approaching a roundabout when I was confronted by three youths.

One of them produced a knife and said, 'Give us some money.'

I was very scared, of course, but I struggled to conceal my fear.

'Take off your clothes,' the youngest of the three men was saying.

I noted that the knife was all that these three had between them with which to threaten me. I got the impression that it was actually a kitchen knife. These were young boys playing at being robbers. Their voices carried no trace of confidence: in fact, I could tell that they were rather frightened.

One of them kicked my leg. I, Fernando Luis of Camp Alpha Zulu, being kicked by this nincompoop! I was not going to be humiliated before these worthless thugs. The other one kicked me in the stomach. It hurt a lot. I handed over some banknotes to them. The thugs kept insulting me; they clearly thought they had chanced upon easy prey.

I said, 'Come on, I've given you the money, what else do you want?'

I felt another kick to my ribs, then a punch landed on my face. Kicks and punches rained all over. I tried to fight back, but these assailants were too tough for me. I started running as fast as I could. For a while, I could hear them behind me, and then, when I got near the beach, I looked back and saw only one thug chasing me. He was the smallest of the three, and he had obviously not realised that the others had given up the chase. This was my chance to avenge the kicks and punches I had suffered. The young thug lunged at me with all his force. I had once done some boxing. I have faith in the power of my punches if not in the thrust of my body. I guarded myself and threw several quick punches at the thug's face. I could hear him squeal as they found their mark. The thug was staggered by this response. His colleagues were not in sight; he was at my mercy. He tried to kick me, but I landed several effective punches and he fell to the ground. The thug was bleeding; he stood up and raised both arms. I gave him another violent punch. He fell to the ground again. I kicked him hard.

He shouted out, 'This is not fair. I am down.'

This reminded me of the insults that had been hurled at me at Camp Alpha Zulu. What this thug seemed to be saying in effect was that I was a coward. I decided to teach him a lesson. I continued kicking him on the head. I saw a large rock nearby. I lifted it with both hands and aimed it at his head. It did not finish him. There was blood all over his face. I hit the rock this time against his chest. He kicked about, like a chicken whose head had just been severed. I was glad when he stopped kicking about. I thought he was gone. I was wrong; he stood up and began to run. This time, I picked up the stone and aimed for his head. It hit him on the back and he fell to the ground.

He said, 'What's going on? You're going to kill me!'

I continued kicking him. He covered his head with his hands. I kicked harder, and was pleased to see his hands become swollen. Then he fainted. I pulled out my belt, tied it around his neck and pulled it as hard as I could. I wanted to make sure that he was completely dead. I could tell a corpse, having seen so many in my time. I was satisfied when I felt that his heartbeat had stopped. It occurred to me that there was a slight chance he would survive; after all, I was aware of how resilient human life could be. To make sure that he would never forget meeting me, I picked up another large stone nearby and thumped it into his head. The human skull is an amazing contraption. I hoped to smash his head to pieces, but it was still intact after I had hit him several times.

After that, I walked home as fast as I could. Had I met any other thug, I would certainly have pulped him into a mush without thinking about it. When I got home, I took a shower and washed the blood out of my clothes. Sayonara was too deep in her sleep to have heard me. I slept peacefully. I had actually enjoyed seeing that thug in pain. I had enjoyed hearing his cries for mercy, I had enjoyed continuing mercilessly to beat him.

The following evening, I went to a samba party and sieved my sins away. I came back home very drunk.

The next morning, I found Sayonara in the lounge painting. She warned me not to go out late at night because there was a strange kind of killer on the loose in Salvador. In the past, she said, all deaths had been the result of knifings or shootings; but now there was a killer who was so brutal he smashed his male victims to death before raping them. I said the last part was certainly an addition. Sayonara said that she had heard some people talk about the body of some petty thief that had been found at the beach near Barra. She was worried for me because thieves would associate my accent with money or privilege. I said I was old enough to look after myself.

I was not worried about the police. I knew that the life of a petty thief mattered little to them; besides, I could always say that I strangled him in self-defence, which, in a way, was true.

Two weeks went by and the death was forgotten by everyone else. I kept on going to the samba parties, but made a point of never moving about late at night on my own. I always took a taxi or a ride in someone's car. One night, I was at a samba party in Liberdade when I saw one of the youths who had attacked me, one of the ones who had given up the chase. We recognised each other, but I pretended not to have seen him. As I danced, I kept stealing glances at his table: his eyes were fixed on me. I rushed out, walked to the main street nearby, flagged down a taxi and got into it. When I looked back, I recognised the two youths standing on the roadside; they had followed me. I was very alarmed.

When I got home, Sayonara was in the lounge

reading the Bible. She had suddenly taken to the Holy Book. I made some coffee and we sat down to chat. In recent weeks I had not shown much interest in Sayonara's work. I had felt that by looking at her paintings, I would only have been reminded of how unlovable I was.

We sat in silence for a while. Sayonara noticed that there was something wrong; I never usually drank coffee so late at night. In fact, I was always complaining that I did not go to sleep easily. I wanted to talk to Sayonara. I felt very alone and desperate. I suspected that countless thugs out there were determined to get me. Salvador was such a small place; I knew they would eventually catch up with me.

I turned to Sayonara and said, 'Do you ever think of death?'

'Never. Why do you ask?'

'I was just wondering.'

'Do you?'

'A lot.'

Sayonara said that ever since her mother had died she hated to think about death. I wanted Sayonara to tell me more about her mother and her past, but she kept it to herself.

Then Sayonara said, 'Nando, you are a very strange person. I've known you for a while but I still don't understand you. Why couldn't you tell that I was almost in love with you? Why does everything have to be so literal?'

I could not believe my ears. Sayonara de Aparecida Lunn falling in love with Fernando Luis? It seemed so impossible. Sayonara said she had learnt from experience never to pour out all her feelings to a man lest he take advantage of her. She said when she had told me that she could never come to love me, she had been testing my resolve. It had saddened her greatly that I made no effort to win her heart. I asked her if she could ever love me again. She said it was a silly question.

So Sayonara had almost loved me; and I was so boorish I had not understood. At last, I was within reach of being loved. I needed to be loved.

Once, I tried to fondle Sayonara, but she pulled away and told me to behave myself. Although we lived in the same house, I began writing her letters. Some of them took me the whole day to compose. I racked my brains to come up with original phrases to describe my love for her. She would reply in terse notes, saying she had taken everything I had written into consideration.

I composed a long poem entitled 'The Bahian Goddess'. Sayonara thanked me for it and said she would always keep it. I longed for Sayonara. I longed to be fondled by her. I longed to feel safe. In Sayonara, I saw all the warmth and love I had yearned for since Tete's death. If only Sayonara could come to love me, then all the slights I had suffered at the hands of Monangolas would be annulled.

I carried Sayonara's photograph with me when I went for walks in the afternoon. I stopped frequenting samba parties and confined myself to the house. As Sayonara came and went, she seemed to become prettier and even holier. Sometimes, I found bits of her hair in the bathroom: I put them in a little plastic bag, which I kept in my bedroom. Whenever Sayonara fried something in palm oil, I would sit in the lounge and feel like a little baby. In those moments, I would forget the SIS, the thugs who were certainly after me, how wretched I was. I would be transposed to the bosom of my dreams.

Usually, I no longer wanted to think of Henrique, or of the SIS. I had by then been in Brazil for six months. I just wanted to think of Sayonara.

Sometimes, she and her friends would take me to the beach. Each time I saw Sayonara in her swimming-costume I felt like rushing up to her and holding her so tightly that we could dissolve into each other. But Sayonara insisted that she did not see herself ever coming to love me now. I began to feel that I was truly unlovable.

One evening, while I was having a heated discussion with Sayonara over the meaning of life, she quoted some Greek philosopher who had asserted that an unexamined life was not worth living. That phrase had been constantly ringing in my mind. Had I ever met that philosopher, I would have added that a life devoid of love is also not worth living. Brazil, I had concluded, had not saved me; nothing could have saved me. Sayonara often talked about reincarnation and said she hoped to be a cat in her next life. When she asked me what I wished to be reincarnated as, I could not help mentioning a flower or some bird that might add a little joy to this world. Given the chance, I would have done everything to clear the pain I had sown at Camp Alpha Zulu. Instead of torturing people, I would have become a medical assistant and given comfort to people. It was, however, too late. The faith I had in Brazil had fizzled out; the evil that had manifested itself so strongly at Camp Alpha Zulu still lingered within me.

I became very aware of my own death. Apart from the thugs, there were the SIS people. I knew that Americo Alves was receiving frantic calls from Alberto Guedes, the SIS director, to locate me. I was certain that one of these days Americo Alves would hire people to come and finish me off. One thing worried me a great deal: I wanted to be buried in a proper coffin. From that time on, I could only imagine my life in a coffin. After all, I could only reach orgasm after thinking of Tete.

One of the things about Salvador that struck me most were the coffin shops; they seemed to be everywhere. I dreaded not being buried in a coffin. I had seen men being buried wrapped in blankets (for the lucky ones) or without clothes. I wanted to go with dignity. As soon as I became convinced that death was at hand, I took it into my head to do two things: begin writing my story, and get myself a coffin.

One day, I wandered to a coffin shop near Terreiro de Jesus and I asked for a coffin to fit a man my size. The shop assistant, a solemn-looking short woman, indicated the most expensive ones. The choice was actually vast: tall coffins, wide coffins and short coffins; lean and fat coffins; medium coffins. There was even a coffin with a glass opening on top. I settled for a simple medium-sized coffin. It was not, however, the cheapest. The woman asked in solemn tones who had died. I said I had a relative who was gravely ill and would soon die. I said I had decided to buy the coffin in advance, in order to make sure that the funeral would not be delayed. The woman said that was a very wise idea. She promised that they could keep the coffin for as long as a month if I paid a little extra. She wrote all my particulars on half of a piece of pink paper, which she attached to the coffin; the other part of the pink paper served as my receipt. Before I left the coffin shop, I asked the woman whether business was good. She said she had no reason to complain.

Having bought my coffin and almost reached the end of my story, there was only one other thing I needed before exiting from this world: Sayonara's love. But Sayonara insisted on waiting for the magical moment when she would suddenly be seized by an overwhelming urge to love me. I kept trying. I never lost hope.

I went to Tida and told her that I was madly in love with Sayonara. I knew she was bound to tell her, which she did.

The news of my obsession with Sayonara went around Salvador. People who had stopped seeing me at the samba parties were told that I was completely taken up with love for Sayonara. Sayonara, for her part, I learnt, kept telling people that she could not understand what made her so special that I should almost become insane for her love.

One evening, I heard moans coming from Sayonara's room. Zeca, the medical assistant, was giving her a thrill. I went to the wall and listened as they worked themselves up to a climax. My ardent wish at the time was to pick up a knife and tear them both to pieces. I almost succumbed to this wish; but I contained myself and started crying. After they made love, I heard Zeca say he wanted something to eat. Sayonara went and got him something that filled the house with the smell of palm oil. This smell reminded me once again of just how unlovable I was. I cried some more. I hated myself. Here I was a big man shedding tears! It then became very clear to me that I had to go. I could no longer continue in this world.

Sayonara was surprised when she saw me the following morning. She had thought that I had gone out for a party that would have lasted the whole night.

'So you heard everything?' she asked.

I nodded.

Sayonara hugged me and said, 'I am sorry. I thought you were out. I almost loved you once. But I still like you very much. You are my brother.'

One evening, I masturbated as I once again imagined myself making love to Sayonara. Suddenly, as I was about to come, I pictured myself on top of Sayonara in the coffin I had just bought. My imagination is as wicked as my soul. I imagined that the coffin was in the lounge, which had been filled with the smell of palm oil. I felt so fine, so secure, that I came at once. I never stopped thinking of the coffin. I had made up my mind

I was going to help myself leave this wretched world. I was irredeemable, and unlovable. There were many people out there who would have rejoiced at seeing me tortured.

On the few occasions that I ventured out of the house I wandered to the beach. I had began to lose interest in the world. In the past, finding young people on the beach at ten in the morning – as was the custom in Salvador – would have filled me with indignation. I was intolerant of people who seemed to have no ambitions. Now, I was not bothered. Many of those young people, I concluded, would pass through this world without becoming as depraved as some of us.

I had been consumed with ambition. I had killed and tortured. Ambition had reared the monster in me; I could not get rid of it. I was a killer, a merciless torturer. I was evil, and I could never be otherwise.

My life is of little importance to the world. I will soon go. Perhaps, with some luck, somebody may come across this manuscript and turn what I have written into a story, and claim that all the events described here emanated from his imagination. I hold no brief for such a person. Perhaps the same person might tear all these pages up, saying they are of little value. Again, I accept such a decision quietly.

I will go, but men and women will bear more babies who will grow up into adults and be greeted by the atrocities of this world. As long as there are humans on earth, there will be many people like me, in whom the devil is so well embedded – who will torture and kill at the first opportunity. All extremes in life, pushed far enough, bring out the worst in us. I do not blame any theory or system of ideas for the evil in me. But I should say that in Henrique, as we became drowsy with ideas, we saw the basest instincts set themselves loose on the land. We were depraved. In Henrique, I just happened to be in an environment where the worst in me was fostered.

In the end, love will win. Intolerance will have to crumble. Writing my story has helped me understand myself, and why mine is not a worthy life. In writing this, I have had to leave out many facts that are of little interest. I wanted to include only what was important in the narrative that would finally give meaning to my life. Writing has also humbled me. I have come to realise that in Henrique, we deluded ourselves with the idea that the glorious future awaiting us justified anything.

Sometimes I feel that of all evil people, I am the least happy because I long for purity. I long for love. As I will never find it, the best course for me is to make a final exit.

As I write this, I have already acquired the pills. I will drink them down with half a bottle of whisky. I have worked it all out: I will leave instructions regarding my burial (on pink paper) for Sayonara and those who might mourn me. I expect to be buried with a copy of *Nostromo*. I will leave the little money I have for my funeral expenses. Some of this money must be used for a samba party lasting all night. Food fried in palm oil must be served. I hope each person will sieve himself or herself into the rhythm of samba. I failed.